DOUBT AND REDEMPTION

OTHER BOOKS BY LYLE E. HERBAUGH

You're Not Smart Enough to Do That
Stories from my life

Doubt and Redemption

DOUBT AND REDEMPTION

BY

LYLE E. HERBAUGH

Published by
Bookstand Publishing
Morgan Hill, CA 95037
4272_3

Copyright © 2015 by Lyle E. Herbaugh
All rights reserved. No part of this publication may be reproduced or transmitted in any form or by any means, electronic or mechanical, including photocopy, recording, or any information storage and retrieval system, without permission in writing from the copyright owner.

ISBN 978-1-63498-115-6

Printed in the United States of America

PREFACE

I Searched For God

I searched for God
In the great cathedrals of the world,
In the temples, the synagogues and the mosques.
I was humbled by their elegance
Awed by their splendor
Fascinated by the pomp and ritual.
The voices echoed from the aging walls.
I asked, "God, are you here?"
The sound of the rites faded
And silence was my answer.

I searched for God
In the byways of the world.
I searched at the beach
Enraptured by the beauty of the sea,
Watching the sea birds soar
And the sunset turn the sky to red.
I searched on the mountain trails
Where the wind whispered in the lofty pines
And the peaks reflected in the mirror lakes.
I searched in the parks and gardens
Where flowers bloomed in profusion
And song birds sang their cheerful tunes.
I asked, "God, are you here?"
I smiled, contentment filled my heart
And silence was my answer.

By Lyle Herbaugh

ACKNOWLEDGEMENTS

To my wife for her patience and support. To my daughter-in-law Elizabeth for her many hours of reading, rewriting and editing. Without her support, I could not have completed the story. To my sister-in-law Helen, for her editing and for her many helpful comments. Thank you.

PROLOGUE

Anthony John Peterson, Tony, was eight years old when he "was saved." He had no idea from what he was saved; he only knew what his Sunday school teacher had told him. He was free from a life of sin. He had no idea what sin was or what a life of sin meant, but it had to be bad because the pastor had said many times that anyone who sinned was going to Hell. He wasn't sure what Hell was either, but he knew it must also be bad. All he had to do was believe in Jesus and not sin, and he would go to Heaven instead.

During the summer of his 10th birthday, he learned what hell is like, in a most real and profound way. An evangelist was to speak at the church that evening and Tony's parents insisted that he go with them. This was not unusual because they always went to church together, especially on Sunday evening. They had been doing that as long as he could remember. The service was a typical Sunday evening service. The pastor led the opening prayer and then they sang two hymns from the hymnal. Following a reading from the Bible, they sang another hymn and then the offering plate was passed. During the offering, one of the church members sang a special song, singing about half of it out of tune. This didn't seem to bother anyone, and the song ended with a round of applause and several loud "Amen." Then it was time for the sermon.

The guest evangelist was a woman, which was somewhat unusual. When she was introduced by the pastor, he talked about how she came to know the Lord, and how God had led her into the ministry. He announced that her sermon for the evening was on everlasting punishment for sinners.

She was a very dynamic speaker. She started slowly but soon was excitedly telling the story. She sucked in her breath like an athlete working out as she marched back and forth across the stage. Her voice rose to a fever pitch as she preached the horrors of hellfire and brimstone. Perspiration stood out on her brow, her breathing was heavy and loud. Little drops of spit flew from her lips as she spoke.

"If you sin, any kind of sin, and you do not get down on your knees and beg the Lord for forgiveness of that sin, dear brothers and sisters, you will reside in Hell forever and ever. You will burn for eternity!" She almost shouted for emphasis.

"You will go to Hell where you will burn forever. The pain will rack your body and you will beg for it to stop, but it will not stop. You will see the burned skin peeling from your seared limbs, but the pain will not stop. You will cry out for God to hear you, but He will not hear you. God cannot look upon sin and you have sinned."

She paused a moment for emphasis, and went on.

"Think about your life. Think about how you have sinned and ask for forgiveness right now." Her voice suddenly became soft when she warmly asked, "does anyone want to come forward and get right with God? All you have to do is to come forward, get down on your knees and ask God to forgive you of your sins. He is faithful and just to forgive you your sins. He will remember them no more."

Tony had been sobbing in fear for the past few minutes and he wanted God's forgiveness more than anything he had ever wanted. He didn't know what sin he had committed, and so he was terrified that he would not ask forgiveness for something he had done. Before the speaker completed the alter call, Tony was out of his seat, running forward to the altar to be forgiven.

The pastor, the speaker, and most of the adults from the church came to where Tony was kneeling. They laid hands on his head and his shoulders and prayed for his soul. They prayed for his salvation and he was saved.

Tony was concerned that his salvation would not last. Could he live his life without sinning again? How was he going to do that when he didn't know what defined a sin? He knew he would have to study the Bible very diligently to understand what it was that God demanded of him.

That night he had his first nightmare about burning in Hell. He awoke shaking in fear, his bed wet with sweat. The nightmares continued for the next twenty years.

1

Anthony John Peterson was born on April 1, 1936. For much of his youth, his siblings lovingly referred to him as an April fool's Joke. No matter how many times he said he didn't like it, the nickname remained. He was the youngest of five children, with three sisters and one brother.

His parents were farmers enjoying the blessing of God and all that the good earth could provide. They had cows and sold the milk, but not enough to be called a dairy farm. They had chickens and sold the eggs, but not enough to be called an egg farm. They raised a few pigs which they sold for meat. They had a few beef cattle that they also sold for meat. Once each year they slaughtered a steer and a pig for their own consumption. With all of this and a large vegetable garden, they had more food than they needed.

Each Sunday they loaded milk, eggs, garden produce, that was in season and some of whatever else they had, into the car and took it to the church for the pastor and his family. They also gave ten percent of their money to the church. The Bible said they were to give ten percent to the church and they did. The Bible also told them to leave some of the crop in the field for the poor to harvest, so they gave to the local food bank. The Apostle Paul had thanked his followers for their assistance to him when he was traveling and teaching, so they understood it was God's direction to provide for the pastor. They deeply regarded these things as their moral and God-given responsibility. They clearly believed that if the Bible said to do something that is what you did. If it said not to do something, you did not do it. No excuses or funny interpretations, no discussion was necessary, only action. If it's God's will then that is what you do. To the family the Bible was quite clear on what is God's will. All you had to do was to read it and take it to heart.

Tony's early life was filled with talk of God's will and God's direction for his life. Most of it he was too young to understand, but he certainly understood that his life belonged to God, and that any decision he would make must be made only after a lot of prayer, and understanding what the Bible said about the subject at hand.

Each evening, after the family was finished with their chores, it was time for the daily devotionals. The entire family gathered in the living room with their Bibles in hand. His father always opened with a prayer of thanksgiving. His dad said that you never opened a worship session with a request. You only asked for something after you had thanked God for all that He had done and for His promise of a wonderful life and future with Him in Heaven.

Following the prayer, each family member read his or her choice of the scripture of the day. All were expected to select one verse for their part in the evening devotional. That way they gave it some thought and didn't just open the Bible and read something. After reading it aloud, each one had to explain why they chose that verse and what it said to them. Sometimes this opened a long discussion about what the verse meant to the others. It was a wonderful time of learning and devotion, which Tony dearly loved. His mind was always searching for information and understanding. It was important to him to understand what it meant to live a Christian life. He was very curious about how God would work in his life, and what he could expect from God.

When everyone had taken a turn reading, it was time for prayers of supplication. You didn't ask for toys or some other item of materialistic nature. You only asked God for his guidance and further blessing on your endeavors. Every request had to be tempered with the phrase "If it is your will." His father had always said that everything that happened in life was part of God's plan, and that He had a reason for everything. Many times, it was not clear what the reason was, but God said in his scripture that He did not think the way we do, and His ways are not our ways, so if we didn't understand something it didn't matter. Only God's will was important.

This was very confusing to a young man when something terrible happened to someone they knew, or when major natural disasters happened. When a tornado tore through a small town in Nebraska, killing many of the folks and leaving others with no homes or businesses, Tony had no idea how such a thing could be the will of a loving God, but his father said that it was, and that was enough for him. His father was the smartest person in the whole world, and he would never tell Tony something that was not completely true.

His happiness and contentment were shattered that summer evening when he heard the sermon on everlasting punishment by burning in Hell. Hell was so horrible, and the distinction between right and wrong was often blurred. If you could believe the evangelist, and Tony thought you could, then every sin had to be admitted and God must be asked to forgive the transgression, no matter how small or how large. They were all the same, because in the eyes of God, sin was sin and there was no such thing as a little sin or a big sin. Sin was sin and that was that.

Tony was concerned about speaking in tongues and being filled with the Holy Spirit. Someone frequently spoke in tongues during the Sunday services, and then someone else would translate. No one knew if what was said in tongues was a real language or not, but it didn't matter. It was the Holy Spirit speaking, so if the spirit chose to speak in an earthly language that was fine. If he chose to speak in the language of the angels, that was also fine. What counted was that someone spoke and someone translated. This was a message straight from God and what was said was important to everyone in the room.

Sometimes a person was expected to speak in tongues to be filled with the Holy Spirit. After being baptized, they would demonstrate their salvation by speaking in tongues. It usually happened after the Sunday evening service when everyone was gathered around the altar praying. No translation was necessary. The speaking in tongues was simply a physical manifestation of a person's spiritual condition. It was God's way of saying, "I love you and welcome to my place." This had not happened to Tony and he was worried that he was not saved. He didn't mention it to anyone because he assumed that when the Spirit was ready, he would be filled with the spirit and he would speak in tongues.

For Tony, it was the perfect way to grow up. He did not have a care in the world. His every need, both physical and emotional, was satisfied by his family. He was dearly loved by his parents, his siblings, and by God. What better way was there to live and to grow up?

At the age of twelve, he was considered old enough to make the decision to be baptized. He did so and on a Sunday evening, he was baptized. Their church didn't have a baptismal, but a Baptist church in town did, so a special meeting was organized at the Baptist church, and Tony, along with three other young people was baptized by submersion. He was now officially "Saved". From now on, the decisions he made were between him and God. He could choose to sin and suffer the consequences, or he could choose to obey God's word and enjoy the fruits of his salvation.

The choices one had to make were not always easy to make, because it was not clear how the Bible regarded some of the things the church said were sinful. Television was considered the "eye of the devil in the home." Movies were unquestionably sinful, because they were all lies, based on the ideas of man. Man is full of sin so his ideas could not be God's will. All forms of alcohol were forbidden because alcohol defiled the body, and the body was considered the temple of God. The same rule applied to smoking tobacco. Dancing was very bad. For a man to hold a woman in his arms, to whom he was not married and to feel her body against his was wrong. He would very often lust after her, and to lust after someone in this way was adultery. Jesus said so very clearly in scripture. Many of the school activities were considered to be a sin, because they were attended by sinners, and to associate with sinners was in itself a sin. You could not avoid sinners in school and at work, or during the normal daily routines, but to choose to spend time with sinners was wrong.

There did not seem to be very many fun things a young boy could do, but he accepted the limitations as the will of God. He carefully patterned his life after the rules of the church, but sometimes he wondered why certain things were forbidden.

By the time he reached high school, he had begun to question some of the rules. He did not tell anyone about his doubts because he was sure they would not understand. By doubting, he raised another issue. Was doubt a sin? He wasn't sure, but it might be, and he prayed often for God to remove the doubt and give him the peace he once knew. It didn't happen.

How could attending a roller-skating party on someone's birthday be a sin? He didn't do anything bad, he didn't dance or touch a girl inappropriately, so where was the sin? Where was the sin in attending a school football game and then going to the victory party? There was no alcohol there and he wasn't going to smoke or do anything condemned by the church or forbidden by the Bible, so why was that a sin?

He had no idea, but if these things really were sins, then by doing them he was jeopardizing his spiritual future, and he ran the risk of burning in Hell. The fear alone made him accept the restrictions, and to live his life exactly the way his family and church wanted him to do. Generally speaking, he was satisfied with his life and his place within the church. But he still had doubts. The nightmares continued. At least once a week he dreamed he was burning in Hell.

When he was sixteen, the pastor asked if he would like to preach at a Sunday evening service. He thought that Tony would be a good speaker, and he secretly hoped that God would lead Tony into the ministry. At first Tony didn't want to, but finally he relented and agreed to speak at the service in two weeks. He prayed about the sermon and something popped into his mind. A Bible verse came to mind and when he had read it several times, ideas began to form. He wrote them down and closely examined them. His ideas were so clear and had come to him so easily; he knew it was the Holy Spirit who was guiding his thoughts. The feeling he had was bordering on euphoria. He had a task to do and the Spirit was clearly guiding him. How wonderful, he thought. It was the happiest moment of his life.

He gave the sermon much to the delight of his parents. All the time he was talking his father had beamed with a show of approval. Several times, he was interrupted by loud "Amen." or "Preach it son." The shouts of Amen were like applause to a performer. He loved it. Tony was suddenly sure what he wanted to do with his life. If the pleasure he derived from the shouts of Amen were from God, then it was clear that the Spirit was leading him into the ministry. If the pleasure was from the Devil then it was simply his pride he was feeling. He didn't know what to think, and once again, he was filled with doubt. How could he be sure? How could anyone know? He struggled with his thoughts and emotions for several weeks without satisfaction. He knew he must ask someone, but whom. He couldn't ask his father, because he would have to admit doubt and he didn't want to disappoint his father. Maybe the pastor, but he wasn't sure how to ask the question so he continued to struggle with the question without resolution. He prayed and asked the Holy Spirit for guidance.

Tony was quite close to his older sister, Jean, and they often talked about things that were important to him. He found that he could confide in her and she would always understand where he was coming from, and was usually able to help him understand what was going on.

He told Jean about his feeling of pride and about his doubts. She explained that she didn't know the answer, and that she had some of the same doubts. Her advice was that he should talk with the pastor because it was the pastor's job to teach the flock and to lead them in the right way. He would surely know the answer.

It was suddenly clear to Tony what he should do. He would make an appointment with the pastor and get this settled.

2

The pastor was thrilled to know that Tony wanted to speak to him about possibly going into the ministry. They met in the church office and Tony didn't waste any time in asking the question.

"Pastor," Tony started, "How do you know when the Holy Spirit is leading you? How does He speak to you? When He speaks, how do you know it's Him and not the evil one or just your own thoughts?"

"Those are great questions with which most of us have struggled. I think that everyone who has ever become a pastor has asked those questions, so you are not alone in your doubt. You are also not wrong to doubt, because in such matters you have to be sure it is, in fact, God leading you."

"That's nice to know and I want to come back to those questions, but first I have something that is troubling me even more."

"Ok, let's start there. What is troubling you so much?"

"When I was preparing for the sermon the ideas came to me so easily. First the Bible Verse and then the ideas of what to say about the selection, all just came to mind seemingly without effort on my part. I assumed it was the Holy Spirit guiding me. Then when I was speaking and folks started saying "amen" and "preach it," it was like applause to me and I started feeling pride in what I was saying. If it was the Holy Spirit guiding me I had no right to feel pride, and I suddenly felt very guilty. I didn't know what to feel, so I felt ashamed. Does that ever happen to you?"

"Yes, I have had all of the same feelings. This is part of being human. You feel things, you think things, and you have self-doubts, but that does not threaten your salvation. In John, when Jesus spoke to his disciples about the Holy Spirit, He told them that the Counselor would be with them forever and they would know him *'for he lives with you and will be in you.'* But we are warned. In first John, we are instructed: *'Do not believe every spirit, but test the spirits to see whether they are from God....This is how you can recognize the spirit of God. Every spirit that acknowledges that Jesus Christ has come in the flesh is from God.'* I think a little doubt is good but it should not control your thinking. Does that help you a little?"

"It sure does," Tony replied, "but the issue of feeling pride troubles me more. I really liked the responses I got while I was speaking. I know that in Proverbs it says that pride comes before destruction, and I didn't know what to think."

"Don't be too concerned about it. You are very young and do not have the life experience to know how to deal with these kinds of feelings."

"What do I do about them when you say I don't know how to deal with them? Will that just come naturally to me?"

"Yes, I think it will. Focus your thoughts on the Holy Spirit and try to follow what He tells you. Remember Jesus said in John *'the Holy Spirit, whom the Father will send in my name, will teach you all things and will remind you of everything I have said to you.'* Don't get discouraged if you don't understand what you are feeling. The Spirit will not let you down."

"Thank you for spending so much of your time with me. It has really helped me." Tony said.

"Before you go, let's pray together."

After a short prayer of thanks, Tony left the church and drove home. He felt much better, and he didn't feel the dread of the future he had had when he went to see the pastor.

Lyle E. Herbaugh

3

The years passed and Tony finished high school with honors. The big question he had to deal with during his senior year was where to attend college. He continued to feel the desire to study for the ministry and become a pastor. Time and time again, his thoughts returned to that first sermon he had preached when he was 16 years old. He remembered the feeling of contentment he had felt while preparing and the sound of approval from the congregation. During the past two years, he had been asked to speak on three occasions, and the same thing had happened. He had prepared each sermon with ease. The scripture and the appropriate comments flowed into his mind with very little effort. He knew it must be God calling him to go into the ministry. The nightmare of burning in Hell continued, but only about once a month.

He had asked the pastor about what to do when he felt he was being called to do something. He had been told:

"If you feel you are being asked to do something, pray about it and then do it. If everything goes wrong, it is probably not the call of God. If doors open and things just happen, it is without a doubt the calling of the Holy Spirit."

I guess that is what John meant when he said to test the spirit, he had thought.

His thoughts kept returning to the Southwestern Bible Institute in Texas, an Assemblies of God school that the church newsletter said was becoming a regional school soon. He applied. In 1954, the school became a regional school and he was accepted as a freshman. *Just as the pastor said, if everything works smoothly, it must be right,* he thought.

4

The first day on campus, Tony met the love of his life. She wasn't that interested in him, but he was smitten. Her name was Elizabeth Millison, from Chadron, Nebraska. Her family was business folk who owned a multipurpose store. In one side you could buy farm supplies and on the other side, groceries for the family.

They had attended the United Methodist Church in town and were very devout in their beliefs. Their family life was very much like Tony's, with daily devotions and frequent worship, but the definition of what was a sin was somewhat more liberal. They could attend school functions with a clear conscience; they could mingle with sinners without repercussions. Jesus had dined with tax collectors and there was no greater sinner than a tax collector, so it must be ok. In a way, it made sense to Tony, because how else could you minister to their spiritual needs unless you met with them, and even dined with them. Matthew was a tax collector and he turned out pretty well.

Tony pursued her with all of his charm and ability. It didn't take long before she was as interested in him as he was in her. They started dating midway through the first year. Dates consisted of school sporting events and attending church meetings on Sunday.

They both missed the daily family devotionals and started a group who met in one of their dorm rooms, and held the same style devotional they both knew as children. They found that many of the students had grown up under very similar circumstances, and were longing for the contentment and security provided by their families. The group grew so fast and large that the school soon found out about it and wanted to know exactly what was being taught and discussed in the gatherings. A faculty member attended the group and talked with several of the students. He was easily convinced that the group was definitely teaching in accordance with the church doctrine and principles. They soon provided a room for the group's daily devotionals.

Both Tony and Betsy found the larger groups did not meet their needs and wanted to go back to small groups meeting in their respective rooms. Others felt the same way, and soon small groups of eight to ten students met each evening for the prayer and scripture readings. During these evening meetings when the group would discuss chosen scriptures, some very different views began to appear. Many of the students did not come from Pentecostal churches, and their views differed substantially from those of both Betsy and Tony. Some of the views made good sense to them and they could see that there was more than one way to interpret the Bible. Tony didn't doubt the truth of his beliefs and background, but he became very curious about the other views and wanted to know their origins and their value to a Christian life. Curiosity and questioning is not always welcome in a seminary, and it wasn't long before his advisor and mentor wanted to talk to him.

One of the questions that had come up in discussions was whether God is in control of our lives. In addition, does He have a plan for each of us? If so, when bad things happen, is that God who caused them to happen? Are our lives laid out in a master plan and are we destined to fulfill the plan? Are some of us predestined for salvation and some not? And can we do anything to change the plan?

These questions suddenly moved into the forefront of Tony's thinking when his mother suffered a massive heart attack and died. He was notified that she was ill as soon as it happened and he drove home hoping to see her before she died. He didn't make it. He spent the time at home grieving with the rest of the family but the nagging doubt persisted. How could a loving God end his mother's life so soon and in such a dramatic fashion? His father and the pastor who conducted the funeral service both gave him the stock answer. Believe and have faith. That wasn't enough for Tony any longer. He wanted to know why.

Lyle E. Herbaugh

5

Upon return to the campus, he arranged a meeting with his mentor to discuss the loss of his mother, and ask how it could possibly fit in God's plan. She was serving Him with all her heart and all her mind, and she loved God as much as humanly possible. What possible benefit could come from terminating her life?

"Thank you for meeting with me on such short notice, but my mother's death is very real to me, and I need some guidance." He paused a moment to collect his thoughts.

"I have always been taught, and I accepted that God has a plan for each of us, and that we were destined to live that plan." He paused again.

"No one has ever explained to me exactly where in the Bible it tells us about this master plan and how it is stated. Can you help me there?"

"Yes I think I can. It says in Jeremiah 29:11, *'For I know the plans I have for you' declares the Lord. 'Plans to prosper you and not to harm you, plans to give you hope and a future'.*"

"Yes, but when I read that, it is in the middle of what God is telling Jeremiah about the Children of Israel. The sentence is part of that story. You take it out of context and then say it about you or me. I find that difficult to accept."

"Let's look at another place where the Bible tells you that God has a plan for you. In Ephesians 2, it says *'For we are God's workmanship, created in Christ Jesus to do good works, which God prepared in advance for us to do.'* When God designed you he gave you everything, every skill and ability you would ever need to fulfill the task he has set aside for you to do."

"OK, I can buy that. God has said that I am to do good work, but what does that tell me. How do I know if I should be a tinker, tailor or candle stick maker? How do I know what His plan is? How do I determine which good work it is that I am to do?'

"The only way you will ever find contentment in your life and find true happiness is to know what God has planned for you."

"But how do I make that determination?"

"The only way I know is through prayer and research. Pray, asking God for his guidance, and search the scripture. If you earnestly search the scripture, you will find the answer."

"God has a plan, but He also gave us free will. What happens if either we don't take the time to uncover His plan, or we decide we want something else for our lives? Does it matter or will He change his mind if we ask Him?"

"No I don't believe God changes His mind just because we ask Him to. I don't believe that one can ever find true happiness if he ignores God's plan. If He has equipped you with the skills and knowledge to be a plumber, and you decide to be a truck driver instead, He will not make you become a plumber, but He will not bless your life and give you the peace and satisfaction you would have otherwise experienced."

"Thank you for your help pastor."

"Before you go, let me make one more point. These are questions you should not be asking. God has given you gifts and skills that He wants to help you develop over the course of your life. If you ask Him what they are, He will show you. The key to fulfilling your God-given call is to seek the Lord daily. Hebrews 11:6 tells us that you can never please God without faith, without depending on Him. If you live your life depending on God's wisdom, guidance and grace, you can count on Him to lead you in the path of his greatest blessings. The truth is that there is no way for us to improve on God's perfect plan for our lives. The sooner you get a hold of this truth, the sooner you will begin cooperating with Him to bring it to pass in your life, and the sooner you can begin reaping His blessing.

Lyle E. Herbaugh

6

Tony continued to do well in school, but was very often puzzled by the teaching of the church and what he saw taking place in real life. He was way too curious to accept everything he was told as fact. It seemed to him that way too much must be taken on faith and not so much on fact. He understood that no one had ever proven scientifically that God existed or did not exist. This left only faith. Faith, coupled with many questions.

He read in scientific journals that the new process of carbon dating was proving that dinosaurs were in fact over sixty five million years old, and that stones were showing the earth to be several billion years old. This was in direct conflict with the timeline given in the Bible, which indicated the earth to be less than ten thousand years old. These discoveries also brought into question the story of the creation taking place in seven days. For the first time in his life, he was faced with a conflict between science and church teaching.

The answers to his questions were always:

"Have faith my son" or "you must have faith and God will show you the truth."

He waited for the answer. He prayed. He discussed the issues with Betsy, and they spent many evenings talking and searching the Bible for the answers, but many things remained unclear.

In the daily paper, they read articles of murder, rape, domestic violence, and deadly storms, which took the lives of many innocent people. They wondered how this could be part of God's master plan. How could hundreds of deaths and the destruction of their homes and workplaces possibly be the will of a loving God? The answer again was. "Have faith."

As they learned more and more about the Bible, another very important question arose. Nowhere in the bible did God ask for a human sacrifice. He told Abraham to offer his son Isaac, but He did not allow him to go through with it. He stopped him and provided a ram, caught in a briar, to take Isaacs' place. Later when the Israelites were living in the Promised Land, they kept returning to the worship of Baal and some of them offered their children to the Canaanite God Moloch. God was outraged with them. There was no human sacrifice! Then suddenly it became a requirement for our salvation that Jesus die for the atonement of our sins. We could not be saved and granted eternal life without the death of Jesus. Why was a human sacrifice now part of the equation?

This was a question neither Tony nor Betsy dared to ask. It went to the very heart of Christianity. Without the death and resurrection of Jesus, there could not be a Christian church. The entire history of the church would be null and void. If this truth was questioned it would destroy both of their lifelong teachings and beliefs. But, somehow, they both knew they must find the answer, or the doubt would remain and they would never be satisfied. Where could they look for the answer? Their position as students made it obvious to them that now was not the time to pursue the issue. Now was the time to study, learn, and have faith in God and the church teachings. They assumed that somewhere in the future this question would be resolved.

7

Four years of study finally came to an end and Tony was ordained in the church in which he had grown up. Betsy wanted to remain in the United Methodist Church, but was not yet able to be ordained as a pastor. They were deeply in love and knew they wanted to get married and at some point have a family. The big question was when. Tony received an appointment as assistant pastor in a church in a small western Washington town. As assistant, he would gain experience and the skills needed to be the head pastor of a church and to guide the membership in the proper ways of the church and of God.

Betsy was not sure where she was being led to go but Tony solved her problem. Tony asked her to marry him and she said yes. They agreed that they should do it immediately and move together to Washington.

It took several days to obtain the state wedding license and to secure the blessings of the church, but they said yes without delay. In the mean time, they called their parents and explained what they were doing, and invited them to come to Texas for the wedding.

So in June 1958, they were married in the school chapel and were man and wife. This was the start of a wonderful life together. They both prayed about marriage and were certain that it was God's will and plan that they be together. And so it would appear.

Lyle E. Herbaugh

8

They spent a week with each of their families prior to leaving for Washington. They had no idea what to expect, or how long it would be before they could see their families again, so every minute spent with them was precious. Betsy was a huge hit with Tony's family, and of course, Tony was totally accepted by Betsy's. Much too soon it was time to say good-bye and leave, to begin their lives together.

With everything they owned loaded in an older Chevrolet, they headed west. They arrived in Western Washington on a June day. It was overcast and raining. Not really raindrops, but everything was wet from a mist that just kept falling. No one seemed to mind, and no one carried an umbrella. They accepted the mist as a natural state of things and went on about their lives. Tony knew he was going to like it here.

One of the church members had a small house that was available for rent at a very reasonable rate. It was small but for two people it seemed to be godsend. They moved their few things in and found that they needed almost everything to make this, their first house, feel like home. During their very first service, when Pastor Finney introduced them to the congregation, he made the comment that they needed many items of furniture and other necessities for their home. They were overwhelmed with donations from the church. Folks offered them beds, living room furniture, dishes, pots and pans, and even pictures and knick-knacks. *Everyone is so generous and thoughtful. What a wonderful life this is going to be,* Tony thought. *I can hardly wait to get started.*

Betsy was having the same thoughts and was completely happy with the beginning of their life together. She was anxious to begin serving in the church in any way the wife of the junior pastor can serve. She was willing to do whatever it was that the Lord led them to do, and to serve in any way the calling required.

Both Tony and Betsy knew they were there to learn, and that Pastor Finney was experienced in guiding and nurturing young pastors in becoming mature in God, enabling them to serve as head pastors in another church. Pastor Finney had been doing this for almost twenty years and had prepared a number of young people to serve in small rural churches in other parts of the state. The denomination had determined years ago that it was very difficult to find suitable pastors for the small communities. These small towns were important to the church. The mentality of the rural folks made them very open to the teachings of the church. These were folks who worked hard and sacrificed to raise a family and to provide for their needs. Hardships were common to them, so if something bad happened, it was God's way of testing their faith and tempering them for His plan. They understood that you had to heat, hammer and temper steel to make a useful tool, and this was God's way of preparing them, making them a useful tool for his service. Where others might cry and feel discouraged, they would celebrate and praise God for his mercy and goodness.

They were both ready to start the ministry, but they had no idea what awaited them. There would be things to come that would test their faith.

9

James Finney was approaching his 50th birthday. His hair was showing some gray but one didn't notice it because of his youthful appearance. His hazel eyes sparkled when he smiled, lighting up his entire face. Tony's first impression was that here was a man who loved his work, loved the people he served, and was a man of great integrity. A man one could trust. He kept himself in great physical shape by lifting weights and running. He had been a runner since high school. He used running as his stress release and enjoyed the time to be alone. When problems piled up, as they frequently do for a pastor who truly cares about his flock, he combined running and prayer. When he was alone, he could pray without interruption. He believed that the body was the temple of God, and it was his moral obligation to keep it in the best operating condition he possibly could. Thus he ran. Running cleared his mind of daily clutter, which allowed him to focus his prayer on the problems he needed God to answer.

He had grown up in a small rural community where his family operated a dairy farm. They milked about 30 cows and sold the milk to the Darigold® Company where it was bottled and sold in Seattle. Some of the milk went into drinking milk, and some was made into the best ice cream found in the state. His family attended church on a regular basis, but was not overly religious. His parents were like so many folks of that time. They attended church because they were expected to. God was something they didn't spend much time worrying about, but they considered themselves to be righteous and upright members of the community. They were Christians, not because of their beliefs, but because they were not something else. They didn't know what a Buddhist or a Hindu or even a Muslim was, but they knew they were not one of them. Thus, they were Christian.

During his senior year of high school, James Finney attended an old-fashioned tent meeting and gave his heart and life to Christ. He finally knew what it meant to be a Christian, and to know the love and fulfillment that came with a commitment to God. By the time he finished school, he knew that he wanted to become a pastor. His family had wanted him to stay on the farm and to continue the family tradition of earning a living from the land. His father knew how little their church was able to pay their pastor, and he didn't want his son to have to live that way. Farming was a better way of life. It had been good enough for his grandfather, his father, and for him. It should be good enough for Jim. It wasn't. Jim knew he needed more, that he was being called by God to do something else, and he had to answer the call. That fall he entered a seminary in Chicago. While there, he met and married Barbara Harper.

She was the daughter of a prosperous businessperson, who owned his own company, selling farm equipment to the local farm community. She had never known what it meant to not have money, and not be able to buy whatever she needed or wanted. She wasn't spoiled, but she was accustomed to having her own way. She had come to know the Lord during high school, and had applied to the seminary to improve her understanding of God and to learn how to better serve Him.

DOUBT AND REDEMPTION

It was love at first sight. Their courtship lasted only about six months. When Jim asked her to marry him, she immediately said yes. They wasted no time, and a few months later, they were married. The wedding took place in her hometown, in a beautiful ceremony in her home church. Jim's family was not able to attend because of the farm animals, which kept them tied to the farm. They were disappointed, but when they finally met Barbara, they fell in love with her.

* * * * *

Their first church assignment was assistant pastor in a church with over 600 members, in a large city. Jim struggled with the responsibilities of serving a community he did not understand. They managed the church the way a businessperson would manage his business. There was something lacking, some feeling he could not put his finger on. He was beginning to have doubts about his calling. Was it really God who had called him to be a pastor? He struggled to find the answer, but could not. He ran and prayed. He pleaded with God to give him the answer, to give him a sign that he had made the right choice. None came.

He finally realized that he was not going to find the answer without some help. He went to the head pastor and explained his feelings, his doubts and his concerns. Not only did the pastor understand, he gave some advice beyond *believe and have faith*, which was so often the answer to complex religious questions. Sure, he told Jim to have faith, but he also made it clear that everyone was the product of his or her environment, and their own experiences. God had created man with a free will to make decisions. Some were better decisions than others were, but all people made them.

"The people we are serving grew up in a different environment than you did," he told Jim "but that doesn't make them wrong; it only makes them different. Remember we are all God's children, and we are all tasked to serve God by serving our fellow man. Try to understand them, and adapt your thinking to their way, and see if that doesn't help."

"I don't know if I can do that. I don't have the background to understand why they are the way they are, and I don't know how to get that understanding." Jim responded.

"I think you do have the ability to understand. What you must do is to stop asking God why, and start asking Him how."

Jim knew the pastor was right. He ran and he prayed, and it was only a few days until he began to feel at home, and to understand what it meant to be a servant to the people of the church and the community. Nothing was about Jim Finney. Everything was about God's plan for these people, and how could Jim fit into that plan.

Jim accepted his role and learned all that he could about the ministry for the next three years. He grew in his understanding of the Bible and he grew in his relationship with God. He was ready to move on and become the pastor in his own church. His pastor recommended him with glowing accolades, and in a very short time, he was selected to be head pastor, or the only pastor, in a little town of Werich, WA. A small town located in the center of a farming community. Jim was coming home to his home state, and to a community with which he was very familiar.

The years passed and Jim gained a reputation as a teaching pastor, and a very successful one. The denomination started sending Jim young newly ordained ministers to teach, and to prepare them for their own church in some small town.

He and Barbara enjoyed their role in the church and in the community. Then Tony and Betsy arrived.

Lyle E. Herbaugh

10

Both Tony and Betsy immediately loved Jim and Barbara Finney. They were people whom you could love, you could trust and someone both could emulate. They were looking forward to a close relationship and a rewarding time together serving the Lord.

As they unpacked their things and arranged the donations from the church, they were feeling very satisfied. Pastor and Barbara Finney had welcomed them with open arms. Not only were they made to feel at home, they were treated as equals. There was no pride or feeling of superiority in Pastor Finney, and he treated Tony as an absolute equal. Jim, of course, knew that Tony had no experience in being a pastor, and that he needed a lot of guidance before he would be ready for his own church.

Tony and Betsy had noticed some things about Barbara that they didn't understand. Barbara colored her hair, and both of them had been taught that a woman could not do that. Jezebel had painted her eyes and adorned her hair, and so it was not considered proper for a Christian woman to do so. She also wore rouge and sometimes lipstick, which was forbidden. Tony and Betsy both remembered the words of 1 Timothy 9-10: *"I also want the women to dress modestly, with decency and propriety, adorning themselves, not with elaborate hairstyles or gold or pearls or expensive clothes, [10] but with good deeds, appropriate for women who profess to worship God."* Both knew that they would have to ask about these things, but the first week was not the time to question the pastor about his wife's behavior.

* * * * *

They had been in their home for about a week, when Sister Yardley introduced herself. It was Wednesday evening about eight o'clock when she knocked on the door. Betsy opened the door to find a woman in her late forties standing there with a Bible in her hands. She was dressed in very plain clothes. Her hair was in a tight bun on the back of her head. At first, Betsy thought she was a Mormon woman wanting to preach to her. The woman spoke first.

"Good evening. My name is Judith Yardley, and I am a member of your church. Could I come in for a few minutes? I would like very much to speak with Pastor Tony."

"Sure" Betsy said, "Come on in. Would you like a cup of tea or something else to drink?"

"No thank you, I am fine."

Tony came in and greeted her. "Please sit down and make yourself comfortable."

She took a seat on the sofa and Tony sat down across from her. He liked to be able to look straight into a person's face when they talked, so they could make eye contact. Betsy sat down next to Judith on the sofa.

"So, Judith, is it alright if I call you Judith?"

"Yes, that's fine." she replied.

"What is it that you would like to see me about, Judith?"

"I have some things I must discuss with you. Some very important things, which I feel you should be aware of."

"OK. Fire away."

"We have some things in this church that are very troublesome to many of the members. I have been selected to bring them to your attention, and to work out a resolution."

"Good," Tony said, "tell me about these things and how you feel I can help. But before you do that, explain to me who it is that selected you as their spokesperson and what position in the church you hold that will make it possible for us to resolve the issues. First, have you talked to Pastor Finney about these things?"

"No. We have not been able to resolve the more serious ones, because, as you will soon understand, Pastor Finney and his wife are part of the problem. They refuse to admit their duplicity in them, and thus, refuse to change."

"What position do you hold in the church?" Tony asked.

"I am not in any official position, but I hold a very influential position with many of the members. Since I arrived here I have persuaded several folks that I am here to help the church become what God intended for it to be."

"You said 'since I arrived here'. How long have you been a member of our church?"

"It has not quite been a year, but my calling is true and I have been busy trying to fulfill my calling." Judith explained.

This is one strange conversation. I wonder if this woman is having some mental issues. He didn't say.

"What kind of calling are you referring to? Did the church contact you and ask you to move here?"

"No. God called me here." She answered rather forcibly.

"God called you. I understand how difficult it is sometimes to hear and understand when God calls. How do you know the calling is from God?"

"Because Jesus personally told me."

Tony hoped that his mouth didn't drop open in surprise. He was shocked and not sure how to proceed. He decided that the best way was to go ahead and listen to her.

"You say that Jesus told you personally. Does he talk to you?"

"Of course he does. Don't you ever talk to God?"

"Sure I do. I pray many times during the day," he responded.

"That's not what I mean. I mean, do you have a conversation with Jesus, where you talk to each other? He listens to you and tells you what He thinks and wants. His direction is very easy to hear and to understand."

Wow. This person thinks she talks with Jesus and He tells her what to do. Anyone I have ever heard about that hears God's voice in their heads is more than a little disturbed and frequently becomes violent. I must proceed with caution. Maybe I should get Betsy out of the room in case Judith goes off the deep end.

"So, it was Jesus who told you to come here and lead the church. Isn't that why Pastor Finney and I are here? Did he tell you why you must do this?" He asked. He hoped that his questions would not be taken as confrontational and set her off. He wanted to keep this quiet and end it as soon as possible. But how?

Judith spoke in a very firm voice, filled with the conviction of her belief that she was right and must proceed.

"Yes He did. Just as God spoke to Moses and told him to lead his people out of bondage in Egypt, Jesus spoke to me and told me to come here and to lead the congregation out of the bondage of sin and into the light of His salvation. I intend to fulfill God's bidding and do just that."

"I don't understand. Jesus said that this church, which is dedicated to serving Him, is filled with sin and you are the one to clean up the mess?"

"You must have already noticed that Jim Finney and his floozy wife are not to be trusted."

"Whoa! Let's not start calling people names," Tony stated quite firmly. "Tell me what is bothering you about Pastor Finney, without the name calling."

"James Finney and his wife are evil people who are living a life of sin, and they are not fit to be pastor of any church. They call themselves Christian, but they are not believers!"

Tony was beginning to feel very uncomfortable. This woman was making accusations against a person he admired and trusted. His concern that he and Betsy could be in danger was increasing. He had to find a way to end the conversation and persuade her to leave. But he wasn't sure how.

"I suppose you have a list of sins the pastor has committed."

"Yes I do. His wife wears rogue and lipstick, and she colors her hair. Both of these are clearly sins in the eyes of the church and in the eyes of God."

"Is that all?" he asked.

"No, that is not all." This time her voice was raised a little. Tony knew he had to find a way of ending this conversation.

"Their son is a sinner who defiles his body, the temple of Christ, by smoking and drinking alcohol. He comes to visit and they allow him to stay in their home over night, and sometimes for a week. They are associating with sinners, and this is again clearly a sin. One must not associate with sinners. The church forbids this and so does Jesus. He told me very firmly that this cannot continue."

"Thank you, Judith, but I think I have heard enough for tonight. Let me look into what you have told me. I am not yet ready to judge Pastor Finney or his wife Barbara. Jesus clearly said in the scripture not to judge. He also asked why you look for the splinter in someone else's eye when you ignore the plank in your own eye."

"Don't take too long Pastor Tony. You will hear from me again."

He held the door open for her and wished her a pleasant evening as she left. He closed the door and almost fell into his chair. Betsy looked at him and burst into tears. She sobbed:

"What have we gotten ourselves into?"

Tony was unable to talk for several minutes. The conversation with Sister Yardley left him with so many questions that he didn't know where to start. Betsy and Tony discussed the accusations against Pastor Finney, and had no idea what to do. They prayed long and hard before they retired for the night, hoping God would give them the wisdom to deal with the issues at hand. The next morning their first thoughts were about Sister Yardley. By the time they had finished breakfast, Tony knew they must go to Pastor Finney, and tell him everything about the visit, and the charges made against him.

* * * * *

Jim had completed his morning run and showered. He was feeling good, as was usual after completing three miles. He was pouring himself a fresh cup of coffee when the doorbell rang. He looked through the window to see who it was. It was

DOUBT AND REDEMPTION

Tony and Betsy. He could see by the look on Betsy's face that something was wrong. She looked like she was about to burst into tears.

Jim Finney greeted them warmly and asked them to come in and join him in his daily devotional. He had already completed his devotional, but from the look on their faces, he knew that prayer was what they needed. He knew that whatever this was, it was the first problem in his young life that Tony had to deal with, and he was ill equipped for the task.

After praying, he opened his Bible to the book of James, chapter one, and read verses two thru five: *"[2] Consider it pure joy, my brothers and sisters, whenever you face trials of many kinds, [3] because you know that the testing of your faith produces perseverance. [4] Let perseverance finish its work so that you may be mature and complete, not lacking anything. [5] If any of you lacks wisdom, you should ask God, who gives generously to all without finding fault, and it will be given to you."*

He closed his Bible and asked, "Did you get a visit from Sister Yardley?"

Tony was surprised that the pastor already knew what was bothering him. He hoped that his face didn't reveal the surprise, but inside he was relieved that Jim already knew.

"Yes we did, last night."

"Did she tell you how evil Barbara and I are?"

"Yes, but that's not what's bothering us. We had already noticed some of the things she told us, but we were not ready to ask you about them. What bothers us both is that Judith Yardley claims to talk to Jesus face to face. She doesn't do it through prayer, but she actually talks with Him, just as if He is sitting in the room. When she started telling us how evil you are, I was terrified that she might slip over the edge and do something violent."

"Let me tell you about Sister Yardley. Soon after she arrived in town and started attending our church, she came to me and told me I must stop sinning and ask God for forgiveness. If not she must do her best to have me expelled from the church. She told me that she had been directed by Jesus Himself to pass the message to me. I called our fellow church in her home town, and they were very familiar with Sister Judith Yardley."

"Is she dangerous?"

"No, I don't think she is. She is very strict in her religious beliefs, but I don't think she is going to start killing anyone."

Tony took a deep breath and relaxed. Betsy was relieved, but she didn't relax. She asked, "How can you be so sure?"

"They told me that she had been talking with Jesus since she was a young girl, and that she had never shown any violent tendencies. I think she was under the care of a psychiatrist for several years and was declared to be no danger to the public."

"Isn't that a sign of mental illness? I always thought that people who hear voices in their heads are crazy, and should be taken care of in an institution," Betsy stated.

"Well, this is not a simple case," Jim responded. "Judith Yardley is a strict fundamentalist Christian. She firmly believes the Bible is the word of God, and that every word should be taken literally. If it is written in the Bible, it is a fact, just as it is written. She supports the rules and doctrine of the church, no matter how restrictive or inconvenient."

"That's the way we were both raised," Tony interrupted. "If the Bible says to do a certain thing, then that is what you do. If it says not to do something, you don't do it. My father always said that life is that simple."

"I think at one time life was that simple but the world is changing and the reading of the Bible is also changing," Jim explained.

Tony spoke up: "I agree that the King James Version used English that is no longer spoken, and many of the words have changed. I also agree that the New International Version is much easier to read and understand, but that doesn't change what the Bible says to do or not do. In school, they cautioned us about using only one translation, and told us that reading the same scripture in different translations helped clarify the meaning and the message. I have found that to be true, but the final message is not changed."

"I agree one hundred percent with that statement, but it is not just the translations that are different. The interpretation of what was written is also changing. For example, many of us in the clergy no longer believe that using make-up is a sin, just because Jezebel painted her face and adorned her hair. We believe it was a position taken by zealots who were in control of the American Christian churches at the turn of the 19th century. Since then many Christians have been afraid to challenge that position, afraid to question whether something is a sin or not. In many cases to question church policy or doctrine, was taken as heresy and heretics were excommunicated from the church," Jim explained.

"So that is why Barbara feels comfortable wearing lipstick and makeup. We noticed it right away, and intended to ask about it when the time was right. I think I understand why, but I am not yet sure I understand the position or the reasoning.

I am afraid it could set a precedent which will be applied to other, more serious issues," Tony replied.

"This is a wonderful discussion, and we must continue it, but at a later time. There are many things you learned at home and in school, that may not be the position of many churches today. Over time, you will be exposed to most of them, and you will make your own decisions about their validity. Now we need to return to Sister Judith Yardley. She is your problem of the day," Jim continued. "She believes she has the gifts of discernment, exhortation and healing, and is ordained by Jesus to heal the sick and to cast out demons. She sees demons everywhere. She talks with Jesus every day, and he tells her what to do. It is her divine destiny to rid the church of evil."

Oh, Tony thought, *this could be a real problem.*

Jim continued, "The spiritual gift of discerning of spirits is the ability to read or hear a teaching or to consider a proposed course of action and then determine whether the source behind the teaching or action is divine, human, or satanic. We were encouraged to practice discernment in 1 John 4:1 where it is written: *'Dear friends, do not believe every spirit, but test the spirits to see whether they are from God, because many false prophets have gone out into the world.'*"

Jim paused for a moment, and then continued: "Her determination that Barbara and I are evil is based on her understanding of 2 Corinthians, chapter 11."

Jim opened his Bible and read, starting with verse 12: "*[12] And I will keep on doing what I am doing in order to cut the ground from under those who want an opportunity to be considered equal with us in the things they boast about. [13] For such people are false apostles, deceitful workers, masquerading as apostles of Christ. [14] And no wonder, for*

Satan himself masquerades as an angel of light. [15] *It is not surprising, then, if his servants also masquerade as servants of righteousness. Their end will be what their actions deserve."*

"Because she was also given the gift of exhortation she feels it is her responsibility to lead us away from our sins into salvation. The spiritual gift of exhortation is the ability to call forth the best within others through the ministry of understanding, encouragement and counsel. This gift equips one to lift up and strengthen others by helping them to move from their problem to a resolution of that problem. Since she believes we are not willing to change our sinful ways, we must be driven from the church."

Jim was suddenly very serious. "Tony, here is how her visit will affect you and Betsy. She believes that since I cannot help you fulfill your needs and mentor you on becoming a pastor, she must do so. I cannot because I am a non-believer, and Jesus told her she must shoulder the burden and teach you the proper way to pastor. Tony, you must be very, very careful."

Lyle E. Herbaugh

11

Tony preached from the pulpit one Sunday a month but his sermons were not an immediate hit. He had not forgotten the sermon on hell-fire-and-brimstone that still caused him to have nightmares. His message was one of forgiveness, love, and acceptance. Tony focused his sermons on the words of Jesus. Love your neighbor as yourself. If your neighbor asks for your coat, give him your shirt too. If your neighbor slaps your face, turn the other cheek. He didn't ignore the verses about sinning, especially about lusting in your heart being as bad as the act itself, but he stayed away from punishment for sins, especially Hell.

Sister Judith Yardley led the charge, demanding that he address the punishment for sin.

"You must admit that sin has consequences, and that Hell is definitely where you will spend eternity if you don't repent. You never admit that demons are among us, and that they must be exorcized if we are ever to reap the full benefits from God." She told Tony following one of his early sermons.

Another time she chided him about not speaking in tongues.

"Speaking in tongues is not a spiritual gift I have received and I don't feel that I should pretend that it is. I have other gifts, and I am trying my best to use those gifts when and where ever possible," he told her.

She didn't really listen. She believed that tongues was one of her many gifts and she exercised it frequently during the services. Sometimes during the sermon, she would stand and interrupt by speaking in tongues, which she would then interpret. The message was quite often a critique of something Pastor Finney had just said. Sometimes it was a statement contradicting the message of the sermon.

Sister Yardley was certain that this was God's way of addressing the issues and clarifying misleading statements, sometimes labeling the pastor's words as lies and untruths.

For Judith Yardley it was all very clear. Jesus talked to her and explained all things, but she must use the gift of tongues and interpretation to make the message clear to the remaining members of the church. For Tony, it was an irritation.

When it was pointed out to her that Paul had written in 1 Corinthians 14:28: *"If there is no interpreter, the speaker should keep quiet in the church and speak to himself and to God."* She countered that Paul had also written just a few verses prior in chapter 14: *"He who prophesies is greater than one who speaks in tongues, unless he interprets, so that the church may be edified."*

"This is not a contradiction," she said. "It is a clarification. Yes, it is better if someone else interprets, but in the absence of an interpreter, the speaker must do so, so that the church may be edified. Any spiritual gift, including tongues, is a spirit-given ability which acts as a channel through which the Holy Spirit ministers to the body of Christ. I was given the gift of tongues and I will continue to use this gift whenever I am led by the spirit or directed by Jesus to do so."

And so it went. Whatever Tony did or said was closely scrutinized. Either Sister Yardley or someone who had been instructed by her came to him to help him recognize the error of his ways, and to find the truth. He was told he must more forcefully emphasize the punishment of sin, condemn the use of make-up by the women, discourage socializing with sinners and many other issues.

* * * * *

Tony never discussed his sermons with Pastor Finney prior to the service; however, they did discuss them following the service. Jim was never critical of the message, only the way in which it was delivered.

"Preaching is just like any other form of public speaking. You must deliver the message in a clear and understandable way, without boring the congregation to sleep," he told Tony on one occasion. "There is nothing worse than a wonderful message poorly delivered to a bored audience."

Tony knew that he must perfect his speaking skills if he was ever to become a successful pastor. He also knew that speaking was only one of many skills he must perfect. The most important skill, of course, was listening. If a pastor can't, or won't, listen to his members, they will reject him and his message, without hesitation.

He and Pastor Finney held daily devotionals, followed by long talks about the members of the church and about issues confronting the church and the community. The two of them set aside time each day for any member of the congregation to visit with them, and to bring their fears, troubles and concerns to the pastor. Some of these sessions were very personal and Tony chose not to participate in the discussions. Tony understood that many folks didn't know him well enough to pour out their hearts to him. He knew that to many, he was so young that he couldn't possibly know how to help or what to do. He was surprised about the personal nature of some of the issues raised. Folks talked about their marriage problems, their problems with their children, and their problems in the bedroom. Nothing in his school training had prepared him for these kinds of things and he was grateful for Pastor Finney's inclusion and guidance. Tony learned very fast, and was a good listener. Frequently all the person wanted to do was to talk to someone, and all Tony had to do was listen. He didn't have to offer advice or direction, he listened and they solved their own problems. Tony assumed it was God's way of working in their lives.

Tony knew he had a long way to go, but he was confident that he was on his way to becoming a head pastor of his own church. God, through Pastor Finney, was working in his life and guiding him in the way he should go. To become the pastor God wanted him to be, he needed to listen to God's voice, to pray and learn.

*****

In their personal lives, Tony and Betsy were struggling. Their income was so low that without the gifts of eggs, meat and vegetables brought in by the church members, they would have gone hungry on several occasions. They talked about it and prayed over it many times. Finally, they decided that Betsy should return to school and obtain her teaching certificate. Before doing so, they felt they should talk it over with Pastor Finney.

Jim Finney understood what they were concerned about and encouraged them to follow the path they had laid out. If they felt that God was guiding them, they should press forward with the plan. They did, and within a few months, Betsy was ready to find a job. She found one in the next town teaching the first grade. She loved it. Working with the small children every day awakened a feeling she had not known before. She wanted a child of her own. She always knew that someday they should have a family, but now she wanted it more than anything in the world, and she wanted it right away. She brought it up to Tony one evening.

"Tony, you know how much I love you, and how much I want to support you in this ministry. I am proud of the way you are growing in the Lord, and I want to be a part of it. But there is something missing."

Tony was surprised that she felt something was missing. "What is it you feel is missing? Is it me? Have I done something?"

"No, no, Tony. It is nothing you have said or done. When I started teaching, I realized how much I wanted a child of our own. It has become very important to me."

Tony was overjoyed with the idea of having a child. He took Betsy in his arms and held her tightly.

"Sweetheart, there is nothing I would like more than to have a baby. I have been thinking about it for several months now, but I hesitated to bring it up to you."

Lyle E. Herbaugh

12

Two months later Betsy was pregnant. Both she and Tony were ecstatic, and could hardly wait for the baby to be born. The first few weeks were difficult for Betsy. She was very sick and started every day in the bathroom, sick to her stomach. She went to the doctor, but he was not much help. He gave her something to soothe her stomach, but it only lasted for a few hours and then the nausea started all over again. At the end of the third month her morning sickness stopped. Two days later, she began to bleed, and suffered a miscarriage. She stayed in the hospital for two days to make sure everything was all right.

She came home and sank into a deep depression.

They had already started shopping for the baby. They had had no way of knowing if it would be a boy or a girl but it hadn't mattered; it was going to be their baby. They didn't have a spare room to turn into a nursery, so they had measured their bedroom to make sure a crib would fit there. It would have. They had spent many evenings talking about how the baby would interrupt their lives and about how to raise a child. They had wanted a child so badly that neither of them had really cared about how it would change their lives; they had known everything would be worth it.

Now God had taken their baby and their happiness away from them. They were left with a deep hole in their being, and neither of them knew how to fill it. Neither of them knew what to say to comfort the other.

Pastor Finney and Barbara tried to comfort them but it seemed so meaningless and cruel to say that it was part of God's plan. Barbara was frustrated with her own inability to deal with the loss. She had no idea what to say or do. Here was a precious young woman who trusted God in all things and who had suddenly had her beliefs torn apart. She had trusted God and his plan for her life. He had given her a baby and then torn it away. Why? Barbara was unable to help Betsy.

If Betsy had not been a Christian believer all her life, it would not have been so difficult to accept the loss of the baby. Things like this happen in nature and it is not unusual. But she had been a Christian her entire life. She had always understood deep in her heart that God was in charge, and His plan was always based on love and on caring for her. Now, she didn't know anymore. How was it possible to love someone dearly, give them the promise of a wonderful gift, and then snatch it away? If humans did that to their children, they would be ridiculed by everyone who knows them. It was not acceptable behavior for anyone. In Betsy's eyes, God had done just that.

Betsy was torn. Was it her fault? Was this punishment for something she had done or said? She could not accept that God would love her and then do this to her. Either God was in charge, and He had done this on purpose, or He was not in charge and it just happened. Could it be that God did not love her? Not knowing and not finding answers or solace in the church, in prayer, or from Tony or Jim or Barbara, was tearing her apart. There was nowhere to turn. She stayed in her room as much as possible. She called in sick at school and turned her class over to a substitute teacher. She cried a lot. When she and Tony were together, they hardly spoke. They had never been so lost in their young lives.

DOUBT AND REDEMPTION

* * * * *

Time seems to be the great healer, and soon Betsy went back to school. She didn't cry any more, but when she prayed she didn't have the same feeling of confidence she once had. She had always believed that God heard her prayers and would answer them, but she was no longer sure if He was listening or not.

Time had mellowed Tony and he was able to resume his normal role in the church. His sermons were well received, and he was regaining the confidence he had felt before the baby. He too, had doubted God, and had questioned his beliefs. He finally found peace in knowing that God worked in ways he could not understand, and probably in ways, he should not know. He stopped questioning. His questions had not helped; in fact, they had only made things worse. He found no answers, and the doubts had grown deeper, along with the disappointment that God would not share the answers to his questions. As soon as he stopped questioning God's motives, and stopped asking God why, he felt better. He was almost back to the normal he had known before.

* * * * *

By the summer of 1962, Tony and Betsy had been serving under Pastor Finney for a little over four years. An opening occurred in the small town of Burlington, Washington. The district superintendent asked Jim if Tony was ready for a church of his own. Jim gave him a strong recommendation. A few days later the superintendent called Tony and offered him the church, if he was ready and interested. He was. When he asked Betsy how she felt about moving and becoming the head pastor of a church, she was concerned.

"Let me pray about this, and I think I need to sleep on it. It is such a big undertaking for us. Tony, do you think you, or we, are ready?"

"Yes I think we are," he answered, "I have been hoping and praying for this opportunity for some time now. I feel that this is the answer to my prayers, and that God is leading everyone in the decision making process. I don't think there is too much more I can learn from Pastor Finney. It is time for us to leave the protection he provides us and step out on our own."

"When do we need to make our final decision?" She asked.

"We have until next Monday. Today is Tuesday, so we have a full week to pray and discuss the pros and cons of such a huge move."

"Tony, if we don't know in a week, then I don't think this is from the Lord, and we should consider our options very closely. Remember, we were told to question the spirits, and even though the district office feels we are ready, we must follow our hearts, and not just our heads."

On Monday, Tony called the superintendent and told him they would love to take the assignment and that they looked forward to serving the Lord in Burlington. They were on their way, but to what? They had no idea what awaited them in their new location, or that events would strain their faith and beliefs.

13

The church gave them a wonderful heartfelt going away party. Almost everyone in the congregation was there. It seemed that no one wanted them to leave, above all, not Sister Judith Yardley.

She had become very fond of Tony and had forgiven him for not forcing Pastor Finney out. Tony had won her over with his gentle nature and his constant praise and approval of the things she felt strongly about. He had counseled her on areas with which he disagreed, but never invoked his own beliefs and preferences, he only quoted scripture, and scripture was the one thing Sister Yardley believed.

Many of the older folks offered them advice on what to do and how to approach life. Almost everyone agreed that they should have children.

"You will make wonderful parents," was the line they heard the most.

Both Tony and Betsy thought that maybe the folks were right. Maybe they would make wonderful parents, and maybe it was time to consider trying again. Time would tell, but first they had to move to a strange town, and lead the worship and spiritual life of a new group of folks. In Burlington, they would not have Jim and Barbara Finney to ask for advice and guidance when things got confusing.

Tears were shed, hugs were exchanged, and they left for their new home. Pulling a U-haul trailer they drove North along highway 99, through Seattle, then on to the little towns of Stanwood, and Mount Vernon. Finally, they arrived in Burlington. When they turned off the highway into Fairhaven Avenue, they could see the church, located right on the corner of Walnut Street, directly across from the Hudson Car Sales and Service.

The church was a small white building with no major distinguishing features. In the rear was a small house connected directly to the back of the church. *That has to be the parsonage, which will be our home for the foreseeable future.* Betsy thought. *This will take some getting used to.* She didn't say.

When they stopped the car in front of the parsonage, the front door opened and a very pleasant looking man, in his early forties came out to greet them.

"Hi, I'm Bob Turley, and you must be Tony and Elizabeth? Welcome to Burlington. Climb out and come on in. I've made some coffee, so why don't we just relax for a few moments, then I will show you the place, and get someone over to help you unload the trailer. Incidentally, I am the president of the church council and senior deacon of the church body."

"It's nice to meet you Bob. Yes we are Tony and Betsy, and I for one, could use a nice cup of coffee."

The house was small, but had two bedrooms, with a full bath near both. *The kitchen is a little smaller than I would like, but it will do nicely*, Betsy thought. *In any event, it was big enough, and when they got their few things in, and their smells infused in the house, it would be home.*

Bob had prepared everything for their arrival. Fresh brewed coffee, with cream, real cream from one of the farmers who attended the services. He even had some homemade cookies provided by the farmer's wife. Both Tony and Betsy were delighted. This could be a wonderful experience for them both, and they were excited about getting started.

"Bob" Tony asked, "How big is the congregation?"

"About 50 total, but only about thirty five attend services regularly."

"From the looks of the town, I assume most of the congregation is farmers. We saw a lot of really nice looking farms on the way up." Tony observed.

"Yes, I would say that three quarters of them are farmers and the others live in town." Turley explained.

He went on, "Some of the folks here don't agree with each other about certain church doctrines, at least the way the last pastor laid them out. We are all anxious for you to get settled, so we can get your reading on some of the disagreements. Some of them are pretty hot topics. I don't want to scare you, but these problems have been festering for some time, and I felt, being the council president, I should prepare you a little before you meet the entire church body."

"Well, I do appreciate your warning. I suppose you will be able to fill me in on what is causing the disagreements." *Whatever they were, Mr. Bob Turley would certainly put his view front and center,* he didn't say. *He had to tread lightly until he got to know all the members and their concerns.*

"Sure, I would love to" Bob responded, "but now is not the time. You need to get unpacked and settled before we get down to business. I have arranged for a couple of the youth members to meet us here and help unload your things. They should be here in about an hour, so why don't you look around the house, and bring in your personal things. After you're unpacked, I will show you around the church. We don't want to crowd you too much, so why don't I come by tomorrow morning, give you the grand tour and we can talk then."

"Sounds like a plan. We will see you tomorrow morning Bob."

"Sure thing. See you then." Bob said as he closed the door.

"Well, what do you think, my dear Betsy? Is it anything like you imagined?" Tony wanted to know.

"Tony, I don't even know what I imagined. I had some ideas of what I would like to have happen, and Bob Turley's greeting fit very well in what I wanted, but the news about disagreements in church doctrine bothers me more than a little bit. I hope we haven't jumped out of the frying pan into the fire. Winning over Judith Yardley was difficult, but settling long-standing disputes between warring factions sounds impossible. It is not something I expected or wanted you to have to deal with. Why can't Christians just read the bible, love each other, and not fight about what it says?" Betsy said, obviously upset.

The doorbell rang before Tony could reply. Three young men were waiting to help unload the trailer. With Tony's help and Betsy's guidance, everything was moved into the house and set in place. When the boys left, Tony drove to the U-haul dealer and turned in the trailer.

They spent the rest of the day unpacking boxes and arranging the kitchen, making the beds, and hanging curtains. They even hung the few pictures they owned, and by evening, the house was beginning to feel a little bit like home. There was still a long way to go, but at least it was a start. When they began unpacking, they found that the refrigerator was full of fresh vegetables, eggs, milk, cheese and two beautiful steaks.

DOUBT AND REDEMPTION

The pantry contained canned goods, fruits and vegetables, all put up and donated by the people of the congregation. Betsy pan fried the two steaks, boiled potatoes, and steamed some greens. Their first dinner in their new home in their first church, was wonderful, and the perfect start to the new life they had chosen. Or so it seemed.

It was around 8:30 that evening when the doorbell rang. Tony opened the door and found an older couple, probably in their mid fifties, standing there. The woman was smiling and the man had his hand out offering to shake Tony's hand.

"May we come in?" The man asked. "I'm Grover Miller, and this is my wife Birdie. We both belong to this church, and we just wanted to say hello and welcome you to your new home."

"Yes, of course, come in, we are anxious to meet all of the folks here in Burlington." Tony replied.

I wonder if this is part of the warring factions Bob Turley mentioned. Tony thought. *We will soon see I'm sure. They seem nice enough.*

"Sorry to show up so late. We own a dairy farm up by Bow, and we had to finish milking and doing the chores before we could come. I hope you don't mind too much?" Grover explained.

Tony already knew Grover was a farmer from the dirt under his fingernails, and the calluses' on his very strong hands. He had the kind of handshake you expected from an honest man with nothing to hide. It was the feel of a man you could trust. He would see.

"How long have you been farming here?" Tony asked.

"All of my life. My grandfather bought the farm where we live about 80 years ago. He turned it over to my father, who later passed it on to me." Grover responded. Then continued "I don't know anything else but farming. I will admit it is sometimes hard to make a living, every year it gets a little harder."

"The economy seems to make it harder for the small farmer to survive today, or do I read that wrong?" Tony asked.

"No, you see it right. There is no money for anything we produce. It doesn't make any difference if it is milk, eggs or meat. The price just keeps dropping. If I manufactured something to sell, I would set my own price and the customer could either pay it or leave it. Everything I have to sell is some form of farm produce, and the price is fixed by someone back east who probably hasn't even seen a farm."

Tony thought it was time to move on to the real reason the Millers had paid them a visit.

"How are things here in the church?" Tony opened.

This was apparently, what Grover and Birdie were waiting for. Birdie immediate jumped in. "Terrible!" she almost shouted. "Some people just think they are in charge of everything. They try to push their views on everyone else and try to control everything. I don't think it's proper for them to do that."

"What kind of views are they pushing on the rest? Are they spiritual and scriptural issues where you differ, or is it things that have to do with the management of the church?" Tony wanted to know.

"It's everything you said. They think that because they are chair of the church committee that they are in control of everything." Birdie responded.

"Who is the chair of the committee?" Tony asked not wanting to seem like he knew too much or that he was taking sides.

"Robert Turley and his wife Ruth are it." Birdie responded.

"Is it Robert or his wife Ruth?" Tony asked.

"Officially it is Robert. He was elected during the all church meeting." Grover responded.

Birdie quickly added, "But his wife struts around and tells people what to do as if she is in charge of everything."

Betsy listened quietly without saying anything. *This sounds like the kids in grade school. How is it possible for mature adults to be so upset by such juvenile issues?* She didn't ask. She had heard of disputes like this in school, but this was the last thing she expected in a rural farming community.

Grover continued: "I don't think it is as bad as Birdie makes it sound, but Robert and I don't agree on several things. I don't think this is the time for me to burden you with such things. I just wanted to let you know that not everything is as harmonious as you might expect. Bob is a smooth talker, so you might want to listen closely when he fills you in on things here."

Tony was concerned that he had walked into a personality dispute; at least he hoped that is was, because if it was a spiritual or doctrinal issue it could be serious and difficult to handle.

"Is this difference of opinion between you and Bob Turley a thing just between you two, or is a bigger issue?" Tony wanted to know.

"It's a little bigger than the two of us. Arthur and Ester Weber seem to agree with everything Bob and Ruth Turley say or do, so it is a little bigger."

"Is the rest of the congregation divided on the same issues, or has it not spread that far?"

"No, it seems to be just between us. I don't think the others pay that much attention to how the church is run. They just attend service. They want to sing a hymn and hear a good sermon. They've not heard many good sermons since the last pastor left. There weren't too many good ones when he was here, but that's another story."

Tony was immediately relieved that the fight was only between a handful of folks and not a church-wide split.

"Who has been preaching in the weeks since the pastor left?"

Birdie's face looked like she had just stepped in something a dog had left behind. She had disgust in her voice as she announced "Bob Turley."

"Thank you for telling us this. I am sure we will get much more acquainted with the differences in a short time. Oh, by the way, what did the last pastor say about the split?"

"He was not a strong person, and I think he let the Turleys push him around a little more than he should have. It didn't seem to bother him very much. He let things fester and then asked to be reassigned to a different church. He is head pastor in Silverdale if you want to talk to him." Grover explained.

"I don't think that is necessary. Bob Turley is coming over tomorrow to show me the church and fill me in on where a lot of things stand. I will probably hear more about this then.

Thank you again. I look forward to a wonderful stay here in Burlington, serving the congregation of God fearing folks."

Tony walked them to the door and said good night. When he turned to Betsy, she looked like someone had just punched her in the stomach.

"Tony, I don't like the feel of this. If we don't handle it right and soon, it will destroy everything we want to do here. Our first time alone in the ministry is going to test our faith."

"Remember Betsy, we have God on our side, and with a little help from us, He can deal with anything and everything. In any event, He has a plan, and all we need to do is trust Him. Things may not be what we want, but we don't know what God's plan is, so we cannot jump to conclusions. Time will tell us, and the Holy Spirit will lead us and tell us what to say. I am very sure of that."

* * * * *

Bob Turley and his wife Ruth arrived about nine a.m. just as he had promised.

"I brought Ruth along so she and Betsy can get to know each other, while we are going through the church. They can look at the lady's things, and we can concentrate on the important items."

Grover is right, Tony thought. *Bob likes to take charge and give direction. That is not a bad thing, but it needs to be watched rather closely.*

Tony was not comfortable with separating the church into his and her areas, and he didn't like the reference that women's issues were less important to the life of the church. In his mind there was no such thing as his and hers in the eyes of God. Sure, the scripture defined the roles of both in the church, but it in no way said that one was more or less important to Him. Tony didn't remember that Jesus ever raised the issue of women in the church. He had apparently left that up to the Apostle Paul to deal with. Tony couldn't even remember if Jesus ever addressed the idea of a church at all. He knew that in Matthew Jesus told Peter, *"On this rock I will build my church."* He didn't believe that the word church meant what we understand today. That concept seemed to be something others created years later. The early Christians certainly needed a place for like-minded people to gather and to share the gospel. There weren't very many safe places for them, so to gather and form what we today call a church was quite natural.

Tony was anxious to get started. This was, after all, the first day of his ministry as a head pastor of a church.

"Bob, show me around and tell me what you know, or better, what I need to know. Ladies, enjoy your fellowship, and we will talk later."

It didn't take long to see the church. Between the parsonage and the main sanctuary was a room, which was added after the original church had been built. It was about 25 feet long and 15 feet wide. Bob explained that it was used for the youth groups meeting room, and on Sunday, it was the young people's Sunday school class. A double door opened into the main sanctuary. As you entered the room, to your right was a raised area or platform. A pulpit was right in the center of the stage. Behind it, on the wall was a beautiful cross. Along the front of the stage was a bench like structure that extended the full width of the stage.

"This is the altar where we gather and pray at the end of each service." Bob explained, pointing to the bench. "We never end a service without an altar-call. People need to kneel down and get right with God on a regular basis. I would hope that you continue that tradition."

Tony thought he detected a threatening tone in the comment. Almost as if he was being given some guidance that he would be wise to follow. *Grover was right. He is a smooth talker, and I will be wise to be careful what I say or how I act.* He didn't add.

There were three sets of pews separated by two isles. The pews were hardwood benches with no padding. *Apparently, creature comfort was not a serious consideration here. It would make it hard for anyone to sleep during his sermons. I suppose that is a plus.* He thought. In the rear of the room was a stairway that went up to a glassed-in-room used for a nursery. On each side of the stairway, were two small rooms used for Sunday school classes. The main entrance opened on to Fairhaven Avenue. It was not an impressive building, but it felt right.

Since the moment he had entered the parsonage the day before, Tony had that feeling of being home. Everything in the church gave him the same feeling. He knew that he was right where God wanted him to be. He had that warm feeling of comfort that comes when you submit your life to God. Everything was going to be fine. He couldn't wait to share his feelings with Betsy. But first, he had to listen to Bob Turley for a while longer.

"I like what I see Bob, it's a nice little church. The thing I like most is that I feel the spirit is present in the sanctuary."

"I agree pastor, but there are a few rough spots that need to be ironed out. As I said yesterday, there are some folks who don't care that much for how things are run. They didn't like the last pastor and were very involved in pushing him out.

They wanted an older pastor, one who had more experience, but I convinced the church council that a young man, such as you, is what we need. My first impression is that I was right. Welcome to Burlington, Pastor Tony."

"Is there anything else that I should be aware of? How is the church financially?" Tony inquired.

"We're doing fine right now. We still have a mortgage payment, but it is small enough that we can deal with it. The utilities are low here because we rely on hydroelectric power from the Skagit River Dams."

"I was told when I took the assignment what the pay would be. I accepted that before we made the decision. If the full refrigerator and the stocked pantry are any indication, I don't think we will go hungry. It may be necessary for Betsy to find a teaching job for any extras we need. Is that going to be a problem with anyone?"

"Don't think so. We understand that a family can't live on what we can afford to pay, so it should be fine. If there is any question about the wife working, I think I can deal with it in the church council. Trust me Pastor. I'm on your side."

They walked back into the parsonage to see what the wives were doing. *I wonder what kind of impression Ruth made on Betsy, and what they had discussed. I guess I'll find out soon enough.*

The wives had prepared a light lunch, and while they ate, Bob and Ruth talked about Burlington and how to find the things Tony and Betsy might need.

"Burlington is basically a one street town. Everything is located on Fairhaven Avenue. Up the street a few blocks is a store, where you can buy real high quality work clothes. They have other clothes too, but this is where the farmers shop for their things. Good quality coupled with reasonable prices." Bob explained, "The family has a store in Mount Vernon and in Burlington, and they are good Christians and very honest people, whom you can trust and rely on. They don't attend this church, but that is fine."

Ruth chimed in, "There is also a department store, a dry goods store and a meat market in Burlington, all owned by a local families. They too, are fine folks who can be relied on to do the right thing."

"Just about everything else can be found in Mount Vernon." Bob concluded. Then he continued, "According to the last census there are about fifty two thousand people living in the Skagit Valley, and most of them rely on Mount Vernon to satisfy their needs. That makes Mount Vernon a prosperous place. There are several food-processing plants in Burlington and Mount Vernon, where the farmers sell most of their produce. Peas, potatoes, and corn are big here. Also all types of berries grow here in profusion. Strawberries are some of the best in the world, and the raspberries aren't so bad either. It is a great place to live and to raise children."

Tony and Betsy knew they were going to love it here, no matter what happened. After praying together, Bob and Ruth left them alone. They both gave a big sigh of relief.

Lyle E. Herbaugh

14

On Sunday, Tony gave his first sermon. He only had three days to prepare, and he couldn't preach the same sermon at both the morning and evening services, he needed two. He dusted off two sermons he had given at the last church, and changed them just enough to make them relevant to the new one. Both sermons focused on God's eternal love and on the sacrifice of Jesus. He avoided any mention of Hell and eternal punishment. Tony vowed that he would never stray from the message of love and acceptance. Christians didn't need to be threatened with Hell and damnation.

Following the morning service both Tony and Betsy stood by the door and greeted each person as they left. Everyone was polite and generous in their praise of his sermon. It looked like every member of the church had attended, even those who hadn't been there for weeks. They all wanted to see the new preacher and decide if they would come back or not. From the positive comments, Tony and Betsy were both encouraged, and very pleased, knowing that they had followed God's call and He had rewarded them with acceptance.

Following the evening sermon, Tony gave an altar call, inviting everyone to come forward and spend some time in prayer before the Lord. Everyone responded. Both Tony and Betsy witnessed their first truly Pentecostal prayer service. It was loud, as everyone raised his or her voice in prayer. After a few minutes of intense prayer, several folks fell to the floor, chanting the name of Jesus, over and over. "Jesus, Jesus,

Jesus." Others were praying in a foreign language. They had both heard people speak in tongues many times, but they had never seen such a simultaneous outpouring of the Holy Spirit on so many folks. Was this the way it was on the first Pentecost? Was this how the disciples reacted on that day two thousand years ago. Were they witnessing a return to that first outpouring that changed the church for centuries? Was this really an outpouring of the Holy Ghost they were seeing? They were both overwhelmed with emotion. They didn't know what to think or feel.

Neither of them could sleep that night. The events of the past few hours were so surreal that they didn't know how to wrap their minds around them. Was this the way it is supposed to be? Was it some aberration of the church? Was this what God wanted from his followers? Doubt set in. Had they made the right decision to come here? Nothing had prepared them for this type of prayer service. They were so confused that they didn't even talk about it.

The next morning they were up early and both were ready to talk. After a couple of hours and two pots of coffee, they both decided that this was nothing to fear or to worry about. If this is the way the congregation wants to worship their Lord, then they should be encouraged to do it. After a while, it would probably seem normal to them. They prayed that it would, and asked God for his guidance and support.

* * * * *

Several weeks had passed since that first service. The attendance had dropped a little, but no one had complained about anything Tony had preached. In fact, his sermons were met with frequent "Amen" "Hallelujah" and "Praise the Lord."

Tony had long since stopped feeling pride when someone gave him a loud Amen. He was sure that any praise should go to the Holy Spirit, because it was He who had opened the ears and heart of the person, not Tony. Tony had only mouthed the words the spirit had given him. Tony was a little concerned that things were going too smoothly. He had expected something negative to happen. After the comments of Bob Turley and Grover Miller, he had expected some difference to flare up and to disrupt the tranquility that had settled in. He was concerned that at any moment something could explode on to the scene. It did, but it was not from Grover or Bob.

* * * * *

Sunday morning Tony entered the church and there in the front row was a very familiar face. Judith Yardley. She smiled a warm smile and stood to shake his hand. He greeted her warmly and told her he was glad to see her. Sometimes a little white lie is needed and appropriate. It wasn't truly a lie, because, for some strange reason, he was happy to see her. He could hardly wait for the end of the service so he could talk to her and find out what she was doing in Burlington.

Following the closing prayer, Tony and Betsy went to the main door to greet folks as they departed. Pastor Finney had ended the Sunday morning service this way and Tony had always liked it. You got some instant feedback on your sermon, and generally, the congregation felt that he cared for them and was interested in what they had to say. It seemed like a good idea to do it here right from the beginning. Today, Tony noticed that Judith stood in the background and waited until everyone else had said their greeting and departed.

"Judith Yardley" Tony exclaimed as she approached. "What are you doing in Burlington?" He was not prepared for her answer.

"I moved here. I will be attending church here with you for the foreseeable future."

"Why? What prompted you to make the move?"

"Jesus told me to come here. He said that you were in great danger from outside forces and false Apostles. He told me to come here and help you ward off the evil spirits. I'm here to do His bidding."

"Judith, it is nice that you are concerned for my spiritual well being, but I haven't seen anything since we arrived that indicates there is a problem, or even a potential for one." Tony assured her.

"You can never be sure. The devil works in strange and mysterious ways. He could be waiting in any one in the congregation. Jesus was very clear in expressing the danger to me, and He has never let me down in the past."

"In any event, Judith, you are always welcome in the church. Welcome to Burlington. Where are you staying? Do you have friends here or are you all alone in this Wild West town?" Tony asked, smiling broadly.

"I located a place to rent before I moved. I came up for the weekend and found a nice place in Mount Vernon on 12th street, just a few blocks from Hillcrest Park. It is very suitable, and meets all of my needs."

"Have you found employment here in the valley?"

"No, but I will. I live a rather frugal life, and have very few needs. I have sufficient savings to tide me over for several months. Jesus led me here and I trust in Him to take care of my needs. Remember he said *'do not worry about your life.... Look at the birds of the air, that they do not sow, nor reap nor gather into barns, and yet your heavenly Father feeds them. Are you not worth much more than they?'"*

"Very true, Sister Yardley, I am sure He will see to your needs."

Judith Yardley shook Tony's hand warmly and said good-bye.

Tony closed and locked the church door and headed for the parsonage. He suddenly realized how hungry he was. He wondered what Betsy had prepared. Strangely, he was reassured by the presence of Judith Yardley. He didn't understand it, but he knew that God worked in ways he would never understand. His role was to accept whatever God gave him for a task, and do the best he possibly could.

* * * * *

Tony attended his first church council meeting a week after he arrived. It was a straightforward business meeting. They reviewed the financial position of the church in some detail, mostly for his edification. Everyone was very agreeable and pleasant. Tony had expected something to happen that would support both Bob Turley and Grover Miller's comments of splits and disagreements in the church. Bob Turley was the chairman, and he ran a well-controlled meeting. Grover Miller and Arthur Weber were both voting members of the council but today there was no disagreement on any issue discussed.

Even though they were not voting members, both Birdie Miller and Ester Weber attended the meetings. Everyone was allowed to express their opinions and join in the discussions, but only council members could vote or make a motion. This, however, did not stop them from telling their husbands how to vote. Birdie was especially firm with Grover, and he usually ended up supporting her position. Members or not, they had a definite influence on how the church was managed.

One month later, the council meeting was not as calm as the first one. The members had become accustomed to Tony, and felt they knew him, so any pretense they might have had were gone. It was now business-as-usual.

*****

The first issue that was opened for discussion was whether to buy new hymnals with more modern hymns or keep the old one and obtain some modern music that was not included in the traditional hymnals. Ester and Arthur Weber both wanted music that is more modern and took the position that the old hymns didn't mean much to the younger members and that if we wanted to keep them attending, we must change. Ruth Turley agreed, and so did Bob, but because he was the chairperson, he could only vote to break a tie.

Birdie Miller immediately opposed the idea of modern music in the church. She and Grover were certain that God was pleased with the music and that an organ or piano were the only instruments that had any place in the church. The discussion was energetic and at times heated. Music in the church was a problem that went back many years. In fact, the United Methodist Church had broken away from the main church because of issues surrounding a new and revised hymnal. Tony and Betsy listened closely, but took no position for or against any argument presented. Tony knew that someday, as leader of the church he would be required to weigh in on the issue. He did not look forward to that day.

15

Arthur Weber and his wife Ester owned a farm on Ball Road, near the little community of Avon. The road was a dead-end gravel road on which only four farms were located. They had 100 acres of good farmland, which provided for all of their needs with some left over for the Pastor. Both Arthur and Ester were devout believers who lived their lives in accordance with the Bible. Both Tony and Betsy found them to be pleasant people and enjoyed being around them.

Ester and Arthur Weber were born in Kansas, where they grew into adulthood. Arthur's parents were not religious in any way, so he did not grow up attending church. Ester, on the other hand, was raised in a church going environment. Though not devoutly religious the family attended service on a regular basis. Ester became a strong believer in Jesus and tried to live her life in accordance with His teachings.

Arthur was a farmer who worked hard, but was barely able to earn a living. When he and Ester were married, they moved to Arthur's farm, hoping the two of them could make a go of it. Mother Nature had other plans and as the drought worsened, they, like so many others were forced to leave their land or starve. Many of their neighbors went to California and Arthur considered following them to the land of opportunity. Arthur began to hear stories about how there was no work to be found in California, and that the native Californians didn't like them and did everything in their power to make the newcomers' lives miserable. After considering the options, they decided to go to the Northwest and headed for Washington State. It was a good decision.

The year was 1936, when Arthur and Ester arrived in the Skagit Valley. They rented a few acres near the town of Sedro-Woolley and settled in. Life remained hard because the farm they rented was very poor land. There was no electricity, no running water, or other amenities. In spite of the hardships, it was better than life in the dust bowl of Kansas.

By this time, they had three children. Each Sunday Ester took the children to a little country church not far from the farm. In 1943, they were able to buy the farm on which they now lived. They moved the family to Avon and for the first time in their lives, their future looked bright.

Not long after moving to Avon, Ester was driving through Burlington when she noticed the little white church. She thought, what a cute little church, and decided to attend service the following Sunday. A greeter met her at the door and welcomed her to the service. This was exactly what she hoped to find in a church and she immediately felt at home.

Two years later a visiting evangelist was speaking at the church. Ester asked Arthur to go to the service with her. He went and that night, gave his heart and life to Christ. Ester was thrilled and Arthur was a changed man. Christianity or religion was what he needed to fill his personal life and to give his life meaning. They had attended the church in Burlington ever since.

* * * * *

Robert and Ruth Turley were both born and raised in the Skagit Valley, he in Mount Vernon, and she in Burlington. Bob's father was the manager of a large food processing plant in Mount Vernon. Although not very religious, Bob's parents attended church on a regular basis. Not because they were believers, but because that is what one did. They were prominent business people in the community and part of their social responsibilities was to attend church. Robert was their only child, and he was required to attend services with the rest of the family. Through the years, Robert accepted the views of his father as his own. He attended church but was not, by any stretch of the imagination, an Evangelical Christian.

Ruth was just the opposite of Robert. She grew up on a farm near the Samish River with parents who had strict religious beliefs. They took an active part in the life of the church and served in positions of leadership in the church. Her father was a deacon and head of the church council. He was also a lay pastor, and whenever the pastor was away, he led the service and gave the sermon. Her Mother had musical talent and played the piano for the services. She also had a wonderful singing voice and would often sit at the piano and sing a special song during the offering. From her parent's example, Ruth believed that if you attended a church, you took part in all of the activities of the church.

* * * * *

Bob and Ruth met while attending Washington State College in Pullman, Washington. Both were studying Business Administration, as it relates to agriculture, hoping to follow in their parent's footsteps. Ruth was also carrying a minor in music. It was love at first sight, and they dated throughout the college years. They didn't marry until after graduation and after Robert had found employment.

They knew they should find a church, but neither of them wanted to attend the churches of their parents. They needed a church where they could step out of their parents shadow and use their own management skills to further the ministry. Ruth suggested they try the church in Burlington. They were warmly welcomed by Ester and Author Weber. They felt the same feeling of warmth and friendliness that Ester and Arthur had experienced. The church became their home, and they soon assumed an active role in the life of the church.

Bob worked at the John Deere Farm Implement dealership in Mount Vernon. He was good at what he did, and soon moved up to head of sales. He was a skilled executive with an uncanny sense of timing. He knew what to say and how to say it at the right time to make a sale. He also knew how to treat the customers after they had purchased something. He knew that if you treated someone with respect, and gave them the service they expected, they would become return customers. The dealership flourished and his income grew. After a few years, he was able to buy the dealership and under his leadership, it continued to flourish.

Bob's religious views were not as devout as his wife's. He attended church and participated in all aspects of the church, often taking a leadership role. He preached when needed; prayed publicly and on the surface was a devout Evangelical Christian. Even though the church was a part of the Pentecostal movement, he never spoke in tongues. Many of the things he did in church were merely keeping up appearances. He knew that his wife wanted him to be involved and to do these things, but he didn't truly believe in them. He was going through the motions and doing them very convincingly.

Ruth was a natural leader, and it wasn't long until she became the leader of the worship service. Like her mother, she had a good singing voice and was ideally suited for the role of music leader. She also became active in a women's ministry, and led the church's community support activities. Both Bob and Ruth Turley were happy with their lives and with the church. Only one thing was missing. Their marriage was not exactly blissful.

Ruth believed that all birth control measures were a sin. Early in their marriage, they had made love and enjoyed it. If it resulted in a pregnancy, it was God's will. Ruth bore three children in three years, and decided there would be no more. With her belief about birth control and her not wanting any more children, their sex life almost ceased. The rhythm system was not considered a sin, so by counting the days of the menstrual cycle, they were able to make love once a month. Ruth no longer derived pleasure from having sex, and this monthly event became an obligation. It was conducted without emotion or climax. Robert was frustrated with her attitude, but decided that he would live with it for a time, hoping Ruth would change her mind.

No one knew of their problems. They presented the face of a happily married couple leading an ideal Christian life, blessed by God, and the community.

* * * * *

Grover and Birdie Miller were the oldest members of the church. They were not the oldest in age, but in the years of attending the church. No one was quite sure how long they had been coming; they only knew it was a long time. They were strict Pentecostal Christians, who believed the church was a solemn place, and the only music should be the piano or an organ, but nothing else. They were often upset by the songs Ruth Turley sang, and were not satisfied with the music of the worship team. They were not bashful about expressing their feelings at the council meetings.

They also strongly supported the position that wearing any form of makeup was a sin. The wedding ring was the only jewelry that a woman could wear. They both knew the woman's place in the church was to be quiet, and in no way could a woman teach or preach. That was out of the question. Less than half of the congregation agreed with them.

Most of the members of the church were only interested in attending the services, being fed a spiritual dinner in the pastor's sermon, and then taking part in a rousing prayer time following the Sunday evening service. They didn't give much thought to the issues that were so dear to the others, and the leaders of the church council. If the pastor and the council believed a course of action was necessary, then they should make the changes, take the action, and move on. They were, for the most part, happy that they didn't have to concern themselves with the management of the church. That was what the council was elected to do, so let them do it.

*****

When Judith Yardley arrived in Burlington, the only people she knew were Tony and Betsy. She already knew what they believed because of their close relationship in the previous church. Unless they had changed, and Judith didn't think they had, she could rely on them to support her, and allow her to protect Tony from the false Apostles Jesus had told her about. Her goal now was to become acquainted with the other members, find out their position on many issues, and determine who the false Apostles are. She knew that she must proceed with caution, because the Devil was a powerful and very devious adversary, and he would help the false Apostles maintain their air of devotion and to keep up the false front they had so effectively built.

During a conversation with Jesus, He told her that the primary focus of her efforts should be Bob and Ruth Turley. They were the ones who were leading the charge against the standard rules the church had long accepted as the norm. They were assisted by Arthur and Ester Weber in their efforts to change the church. Jesus did not; however, tell her how to proceed or when to confront the enemy. She assumed that at some future date, Jesus would make things clear, and outline a course of action for her. She would wait, not patiently, but she would continue to gather information, and wait for Jesus to provide instructions.

Since Grover and Birdie Miller were the oldest members of the church, they were her first contacts. After a short conversation, Judith knew that the Millers were strong supporters of the same positions she believed in. Grover and Birdie Miller would be her allies in the fight against evil and sin within the congregation. She knew she must ask Jesus about them the next time she talked with him.

*****

As Tony and Betsy became more and more acquainted with the members and began to understand their desires and beliefs, their concern increased. They could see that unless they took some action, a major disagreement would erupt, and split the church. The big question was what action should they take?

What should the position of the church be in the changing world, and the changing attitudes of the country? Are the old ways the right ways? Is change in the church doctrines a bad thing? They knew that doctrinal issues could not, and should not, be changed by a local congregation. If they felt strongly about a doctrine, and the majority of the members agreed, then it would be fitting and proper to address them to the denomination. Lesser issues; however, needed to be addressed and a determination made as to how things should be done. Many people talked about something being church doctrine, when in fact, what they were addressing were procedural issues, and had little to do with actual church doctrine. These were the things Tony believed were his responsibility to address. Now he had to determine a course of action. Only prayer would help him make the decisions that faced him. So he prayed.

16

In February 1964, it had been four years since the miscarriage and Tony wanted to try again. He was afraid to bring it up to Betsy, because of the problems she had had the last time, and he didn't want to put her through such mental anguish again. They were watching television one evening when Betsy raised the subject.

"Tony my dear," she started, "how do you feel about having a child?"

"I would love it, but are you ready to try again?"

"Yes."

"You're sure?" he asked, "Really sure?"

"Yes Tony, I have thought about it for several months now, and I have prayed every day, asking God for his guidance."

"Me too." He quickly replied.

"Then it's settled." Betsy stated, "And we can start trying right now, this very moment."

She moved closer to Tony, wrapping her arms around his neck, she kissed him with passion.

"I mean right now." She whispered.

Three weeks later, she missed her period, and the doctor told her that she was pregnant. Tony cried when she told him the news, he was so happy. This time was going to be different, and they were going to have a baby boy. Betsy said it would be a little girl, but it really didn't matter to either of them, they just wanted a baby.

Things went smoothly for the first three months. Betsy's morning sickness was not as bad as the first time and she was feeling confident that it was going to work. During her routine visit to the doctor, he had listened to the baby's heartbeat and told her it was nice and regular. Then he smiled real big and said,

"Betsy, I hear two hearts beating in there. I think you are going to have twins."

She was overjoyed. "That's wonderful doctor, we get two for the price of one. That's a good deal, any way you look at it. I can't wait to tell Tony."

Tony was also thrilled at the thought of having two babies at the same time. Maybe it would be a boy and a girl, then they both would get what they wanted, and there would be no disappointment.

The months flew by and Betsy grew quite large. After the first few weeks, the morning sickness became less and less frequent and the pregnancy grew easier. Both Tony and she enjoyed placing their hands on Betsy's belly and feeling the babies move and kick. Sometimes one of the babies would push against a nerve, and Betsy would turn white from the pain. Every time it happened, Tony would be alarmed, thinking something was wrong.

They went to the local library in Mount Vernon, and found several books with names of both boys and girls. They had to pick two of each sex, because there was no way of knowing what sex the babies would be. What a chore it became. They spent many evenings trying to decide. Each evening they were sure they had made a decision, only to wake up the next day and not feel very secure in their choices.

Their first consideration was biblical names. Names like Seth, Joseph, Isaac, Peter and Paul, also Ruth, Ester, Mary and Martha, were all put on the table and discarded. After exhausting a long list of names, and not finding two they could agree on, they moved on to non-biblical ones.

They also shopped for what they would need to support twins. Two cribs, two strollers, two of everything. They didn't care if the colors were blue for a boy and pink for a girl. They bought whatever they thought was cute enough for their babies, regardless of the color. The wonderful gift from God of twins made them both happy beyond anything they had ever imagined. They were certain it was a gift from God, because neither of them had twins in their family. None as far back as they could trace.

When Betsy went into labor, they still had not firmly decided on what to call the babies. It was November 19, 1964, when the contractions started. They had the bags packed and ready to go. Tony drove her to the Skagit Valley Hospital, in Mount Vernon, and at 10:40 pm, a little girl was born, followed just minutes later, by a boy. Their prayers had been answered, a boy and a girl. What could be better than that?

"Now, what do we name them?" Betsy asked. Both babies had been cleaned up, wrapped in swaddling clothes, and were lying in her arms. Tony stood by the bed and couldn't imagine that life could get any better. Lying there in the hospital bed was his wonderful loving wife, a son and a daughter. He submitted a prayer of thanks to God, because he totally believed such good fortune could only come from a loving God.

Tony replied that he liked Carol Ann for the girl, but wasn't sure about the boy. Betsy wanted to call him Martin

Alexander, and Tony quickly agreed. Both names had been high on their list of possible names, and after seeing the babies, the two names somehow seemed right.

And so it was. Martin Alexander Peterson and Carol Ann Peterson, were welcomed into the world, and dedicated to God and to his service.

Betsy and the babies stayed in the hospital for four days, during which time Betsy was counseled on nursing the infants. The medical opinion was that nursing was not in the best interest of the babies, and with two to feed, it would be almost impossible. Betsy was given a list of things needed to mix the formula and to sterilize the equipment required to bottle-feed them. Tony was able to find everything they needed at Payless Drug store. They were ready to bring their children home. Life was good and everything was wonderful.

* * * * *

Things went right on schedule. The first few weeks neither of them was able to sleep through the night. Babies have their own schedule, and they sleep when they are comfortable, but if the diaper is wet or the tummy is empty, they wake up and cry. Like it or not, one of the parents must get out of bed and take care of them. In this case, both parents were required. During the days, Betsy could manage them both. She settled into a routine; make the formula for the day, sterilize the bottles, fill them and store them in the refrigerator. She filled the washing machine with cloth diapers, and then hung them in the bathroom to dry. If the weather was good, she hung the diapers out on the clothesline to dry. With cooking, keeping house and caring for the twins, Betsy was frequently exhausted by evening. Tony took over the last feeding of the day, changed the twins into their pajamas, and then put them to sleep. He had a large oversized sweater which he used. He reclined on the sofa, placed the babies on his chest, face down, and buttoned the sweater over the two. He somehow knew that they drew comfort from hearing his heartbeat, and from his warmth, because they immediately went to sleep. A bond was formed between father and children, which would last a lifetime and would become very important in the difficult years to come.

As the children grew so did the problems. Money was in short supply, and they found it more and more necessary to rely on the generosity of the congregation. Betsy considered returning to teaching, and even went so far as to apply at Lincoln School in Mount Vernon. Then she changed her mind because she couldn't stand the idea of being away from the twins. Every evening, during their daily devotional, they prayed for wisdom, for God to show them His will and His plan for them. The answer was never clear, but Betsy believed that her reluctance to go to work was a signal from God, that she should stay home and be a full time mother to their children.

The evening news was even more disturbing to them both. Every evening there was news of social issues that would shape the world awaiting their children. There were race riots, and demonstrations in the south. There were reports of police brutality, and horrific treatment of the marchers in Selma, Alabama, and throughout the south. In California, things were worse. The young people of the country were rebelling against the religious and moral standards that made this country strong and a wonderful place to live. To Tony and Betsy, it seemed that the youth of the country had completely lost their way.

Flower Power coupled with a free love culture, undermined everything Tony and Betsy believed in.

They could understand the anti-war movement and in many ways supported it, but they could not understand the looting and destruction of personal property that followed so many of the demonstrations. Nothing made sense to them. They continued to pray for wisdom, and for guidance. Both began to doubt the wisdom of having the children. Into what kind of a world did they bring their children? What future awaited them with everything that was happening?

Of the many movements in California, the one that worried them the most was the Jesus Freaks. This group had discovered The Aquarian Gospel of Jesus the Christ; touted as the Philosophic and Practical Basis of the Religion of the Aquarian Age of the World, and of the Church Universal. This gospel told of the life of Jesus from birth to death. It tells of his years in Tibet and India, where He studied under the great Masters of the Hindu religion. It tells of how he developed into a great Yoga Master, and how this training formed his thoughts and beliefs, and prepared Him for His ministry and for His death. Betsy and Tony believed this was a false gospel written by Satan to lead children away from the true gospel and Jesus Christ.

The world in which the twins would grow up would be a very different world from the one that had formed their parents and grandparents lives and beliefs. These two young children would face decisions and obstacles their parents could not even imagine. The only course Tony and Betsy could take was to pray diligently and to teach the children the same religious and moral things they had been taught. When they reached adulthood, they would have to make the decisions for themselves. And so it was.

Lyle E. Herbaugh

17

Life in the Burlington church was returning to normal. Tony was not sure what could be considered normal, but the disagreement between the members had mellowed somewhat after an incident that happened during one Sunday evening service.

Shortly after Judith Yardley arrived in Burlington, she began to gather like-minded folks together to oppose issues and actions, which they believed, were pushing the church in the wrong direction. They opposed what they called the liberal pathway to Hell. They openly challenged any member of the congregation who thought otherwise. It was open warfare between the pursuers of change, Bob and Ruth Turley with Ester and Arthur Weber, and those who argued that nothing in the church should change, led by Judith Yardley and Grover and Birdie Miller. They believed that it is God's will and that He is satisfied with the way things have been for decades,

They opposed each other over issues that both Tony and Betsy thought to be trivial: Should there be coffee and a social time following the Sunday morning service. Should there be a short time at the start of the service for everyone to meet and greet those sitting close to them.

The argument for the change was that both issues drew the members closer together, and enhanced the fellowship.

Those opposed said that the greeting period disrupted the solemn worshipful atmosphere in the church, and that the social time was bringing things of the world into the church.

This was based on 1 John 2:15: *"Do not love the world or the things in the world. If anyone loves the world, the love of the Father is not in him."*

The arguments disturbed Betsy, and she could only marvel at the level of passion each side showed about issues Betsy considered quite unimportant. She only expressed her concerns to Tony, and never took sides in the public discussions which took place during the council meetings. The disagreements were exacerbated by the fact that Ruth Turley and Judith Yardley did not like each other, and did not hide their contempt for the other.

Following a heated debate in a council meeting, a motion was made to initiate a social hour following the Sunday morning service. The motion passed. That was quickly followed by a second motion to initiate a period of greeting at the start of the Sunday morning service. It also passed. Judith and the Miller family were not happy, but they conceded to the vote. A few weeks after these two motions were put into effect, both parties admitted that they had been wrong and that they rather liked the changes.

Tony was thrilled by the news. *At last,* he thought, *we can agree on something.* The peace didn't last long, and by the next month's council meeting another issue had surfaced. Ruth Turley changed the order of worship without discussing it with anyone, not even Tony. She selected music to sing that was not in the hymnal, and she played her guitar to accompany the song. Even though the song had wonderful lyrics, it was not in the hymnal and the opposition argued that it had no place in the church. Grover and Birdie Miller were outraged that Ruth had done this without them and the church council knowing about it.

At the end of the service, Birdie was upset when she shook hands with Tony. "Did you know that woman was going to do that?" She wanted to know.

"No I didn't know about it. She is; however, in charge of the music portion of worship, so I am sure she felt that it was within the purview of her responsibilities." He replied.

"Well it surely is not! You must nip this in the bud before it grows into something bigger."

"Thank you Birdie, for sharing your views with me." Tony replied, and turned to the next person waiting to shake his hand.

He was a little agitated that Ruth had not cleared it with him. She had to know how important the music was to many of the older members, and she had been there for the council meeting when it was discussed. Tony knew that he needed to discuss it with her, but it would be difficult, because it was a very beautiful song and the words had brought tears to his eyes. In fact, he actually liked the idea of singing some younger more modern music in the service. He would contact her and see what she had in mind, and how far she was planning to take it.

Ruth apologized to Tony for not having cleared the song with him before she included it in the worship time, but she did feel that it was her responsibility to plan and conduct the music part of the worship. Tony agreed that it was within her authority, but that he was responsible for the overall welfare of the congregation, and in reality he should approve major changes in how the service was conducted.

Ruth agreed with Tony, and for the most part always cleared her ideas with him prior to the service. With prior knowledge of events, he could smooth the waters with those who might oppose any changes. It worked well, and Tony was able to keep everything flowing rather smoothly. Occasionally disagreements did surface but they were discussed at the church council meetings. In most cases, the council was able to reach a solution that was agreeable to all concerned.

Over the next year, they resolved to allow the young people of high school age to attend school functions and thereby associate with sinners. This made their lives much simpler, eased some of the stress of being a Christian teenager. Most of the youth gave Tony the credit, and from then on, hung on every word he spoke. They allowed Ruth to continue to incorporate more and more modern music into the Sunday morning services, again much to the delight of the youth.

Word spread around the valley that something was happening at the church in Burlington. Every week Tony saw new faces in the pews. He greeted each one and welcomed them to the service. Under Tony's leadership, the church grew rapidly.

An important crisis erupted several days after the church council could not agree if it was proper for women to wear makeup and jewelry other than her wedding band. Bob Turley, supported by Ruth, Ester, and Arthur, argued strenuously that it should be allowed, and that it was within the authority of the council to allow the change. Judith Yardley was certain that this was against God's law and against the bylaws of the denomination. She was so opposed to the idea that she told the council that this was the work of Satin and his demons. Birdie and Grover Miller were not so adamant; however, they did think it must be presented to the denomination for their approval. For them it was not clear if makeup and jewelry were doctrinal issues or not, but at least they should ask the question. The meeting ended without resolution.

The following Sunday evening, Tony was in the middle of his sermon when suddenly Judith Yardley stood up and asked Tony to stop, because there was something she had been instructed by Jesus to perform. Tony watched in horror as Judith walked over to where Bob Turley was sitting, and placed her hands on his head. In a loud voice, she proclaimed:

"In the name of Jesus I demand you to come out of this person. Release him now, in the name of Jesus. You demons of the Devil have no authority here. Leave him now, I command you in the name of Jesus."

Bob didn't oppose her at all. He sat there with a contented look on his face and waited to see what would happen next. He didn't seem at all concerned about what was happening.

Judith started speaking in another tongue, and ranting. Her right foot was tapping on the floor in rhythm with her ranting. Her voice became high pitched and louder, until she was almost screaming. Then she stopped. She collapsed into the pew, exhausted from the effort, and proclaimed in a loud voice: "It is finished."

Tony abandoned his sermon and called everyone to the altar for prayer.

* * * * *

Betsy was in tears, horrified with what had just happened. She was still crying when they returned to the parsonage. "Tony, what was that?" She wanted to know, "I knew that Judith contends that she has the authority to cast out demons, but Bob Turley. What was she thinking?"

Tony couldn't answer for several minutes. Before he could say anything, Betsy asked, "Do you think she believes that Bob was Demon possessed, and that she has cast it out of him? That was the most terrifying thing I have ever seen, inside or outside a church. What are you going to do? Do you have any idea how to handle a thing like this? I surely don't have a clue."

"No Betsy, I don't know how to handle this. I know that the Lord surely knows, and I must rely on His guidance. I know the Holy Spirit will give me the wisdom to deal with anything that comes from this experience. Remember that Jesus told his disciples that a Comforter would come, who would bring to remembrance everything He had said. I know I am not quoting that correctly, but I know I can rely on the Holy Spirit for guidance."

With that, they turned off the lights and went to bed. Neither of them slept for several hours.

*****

Several weeks later, Judith Yardley dropped in to see Tony in his office. She was very calm and appeared almost serene. She smiled warmly and asked if she could sit down and talk for a few minutes.

"Pastor Tony," she started, "I am sorry things happened the way they did, but I was led by Jesus to perform the exorcism at that moment. I never intended to disrupt the sermon, but I must do what I am told to do, so I acted."

"Yes Judith, go on."

"Jesus spoke to me yesterday evening. I have finished my task here in Burlington. I have protected you from the demon possessed, and have identified the false Apostles in the church. Now you must deal with Bob Turley, or answer to God."

"Did Jesus tell you anything else?" Tony asked.

"Yes He did. He assured me the changes that are taking place within the church are His will and are part of his divine plan. Now I must explain to Grover and Birdie that these changes are what God wants, and try to bring them some comfort and help them deal with their doubts. I must make them understand."

"What are your plans? Will you be staying here in Burlington, or moving on. If my memory serves me right, it has been almost four years since you arrived."

"Yes it has been that long. We have made an awesome team, you and I, and have furthered the work of the Lord during that time."

Wow, your idea of awesome team is a little different from mine. Tony didn't say.

Judith continued. "Yes, I will stay here in Burlington for a while. Jesus told me that I can expect some further guidance, but He did not give me a time frame or a schedule. Until that happens, I shall continue to support any and all decisions you must make. I must continue to support and protect you and Betsy, in any way God leads me."

Tony was not sure her revelation and pledge of support was a blessing or a curse, but he would continue to treat Judith with respect and dignity as long as she attends the church. He thanked her, and smiled when she left.

That evening Tony told Betsy of his conversation with Judith. When he finished Betsy remarked, "Wow that was quite a revelation Judith made. After fighting so hard to prevent the changes, she now supports everything you are trying to do. We both knew that it was God leading us to make the changes, but it took a private conversation with Jesus to convince Judith. Tony, I sometimes wonder about her mental stability."

"I agree with you, but I must assume that the change in her attitude was the work of the Holy Spirit. No matter what caused the shift, I am pleased and relieved that she is now on our side. It will make our work much easier, especially if she can convince Grover and Birdie."

* * * * *

Sunday morning service ended and Tony was greeting folks as they left. Bob Turley approached Tony and asked if he could meet with him on Tuesday. He needed about an hour of Tony's time.

"Of course you can. What time is good for you?" Tony asked.

"Around 10 would be perfect for me," Bob replied.

"Good, I'll block out the time on my calendar for you. What is it that you need to discuss?"

"It's very personal, and I don't want to say anything here where someone might overhear." Bob whispered.

"That's fine. I'll see you on Tuesday at 10.

"Thanks Tony."

I wonder if this has anything to do with Judith and the attempted exorcism. Tony thought. *I guess I'll find out on Tuesday.*

Bob Turley arrived at exactly 10 am. They exchanged the ritual niceties and then Tony asked:

"Bob, what brings you here on a work day? You said it was rather personal, so I know it is important to you. Let's hear it."

"Tony" Bob started, "Let me talk for a while and don't interrupt with advice or comment until I have unloaded what's on my heart."

"Sure Bob, I'm listening."

"As you may have noticed, Ruth and I are having some problems. All is not love and roses in our relationship. It has been building for some time now, and I don't know exactly where to start."

He paused for what seemed like forever. Then he started again.

"I guess I need to start at the beginning, but first I must tell you that I am considering divorcing Ruth."

Tony didn't know what to say, and he had agreed to keep silent, so he said nothing. *How is this possible?* He didn't ask.

"It started not long after we got married. We had, what I thought was a good sex life. We made love quite often, but Ruth does not believe in the use of any birth control methods, which resulted in having all three of our children in the first three years. After the third child was born, Ruth explained that she was not going to have any more children, and that was that. I couldn't argue, having seen the pain and sickness that is part of childbearing.

We agreed that we should not have any more children, but we did not agree on the method that we would use to prevent this from happening. Ruth is very firm in her position that the only way to manage this is to use the rhythm method. We count the days in her menstrual cycle and at the appropriate time when she cannot get pregnant; we have sex. That's only once a month."

Bob paused to gather his thoughts, and started again.

"This lack of affection has caused me to sin. Jesus told us that to lust after another woman was committing adultery. Well, I look at other women and sometimes I lust after them. There is a young woman who works in the company whom I find very attractive. She is in her mid twenties and is a very warm and generous person. By necessity, we see each other every day and must work very closely on a number of things. She seems to like what she sees in me and I think she is also physically attracted to me. I often think of her and wonder what it would be like. I also think of her when I masturbate. Yes, I do that. I don't know of any other way to relieve the pressure that builds up in my groin. I know what Jesus said about the subject, and I also know what Paul wrote about abstinence, but it doesn't help me and it doesn't work for me."

Bob sat there for a moment in silence. His eyes were filled with tears. Tony started to say something, but Bob raised his hand and shook his head no.

"It says somewhere in the New Testament that a wife should submit to her husband, and do his bidding, and I feel that includes satisfying his sexual needs. Ruth refuses to do that for me, and I don't know what to do about it. I know that there is little you can do to help me with this problem, but I had to tell someone. Keeping it all bottled up inside was driving me crazy."

Bob looked away for a moment, then asked: "Am I wrong about this Tony? Is god going to hold me responsible for something that is not my fault? I don't know what to think or do."

Tony's first thoughts were that he didn't want to hear about Bob Turley's sex life, much less give him advice on how to deal with the situation. It took a moment for him to get his thoughts together.

"Bob, first let me say that I cannot know what God will do. I do know that divorce is a big step, which will have a profound effect on your lives. It is not something to be taken lightly. I know you do not take it lightly or you would not be here asking me for my advice."

He paused for another moment then added, "I am not a trained marriage counselor. I am your pastor and I should be able to help you, but I don't know what to say or do. My best advice to you is to find a good Christian marriage counselor. I have the name and phone number of someone who might be able to help you. She is a woman with years of experience. Please ask Ruth if she will go with you and meet with her."

"I doubt that Ruth will be willing to go with me. She doesn't know that I am thinking of divorcing her, and I have never told her how hard it is to exist without love in my life. I need to think about this a little deeper and talk to Ruth about my feelings. Maybe it will help. Thank you Tony, I don't think I could have kept this to myself any longer. One other thing I need to know. Can I continue in my position as deacon in the church?"

"I see no reason for you to change anything until this has played itself out in your life, then we must make the judgment at that time. Bob, I would like to pray with you before you go."

They both prayed for guidance and for wisdom. When they were finished, they shook hands and Bob left. It was very clear to Tony that he had been of little help to Bob, and he felt bad about it. But he truly did not know how to deal with the entire issue. He thought about it for the rest of the day, and by the time he got home in the evening, his frustration level was quite high. Betsy knew something was wrong the moment he came in the door.

"Did you have a bad day today? She asked.

"Yes. Bob Turley came to see me this morning and I was not able to help him with his problem. I can't tell you about our discussions, but he told me about his sex life in great detail. I didn't want to hear about it, but I had to listen to him. Betsy, I don't want to hear about his sex life. I don't know if God will hold me accountable for not caring, but his sex life is between him and Ruth. I am the pastor, but I am not a sex counselor. I know what the bible says about lusting, about adultery, about fornication, and numerous other practices including divorce, but I don't know how to tell someone what to do when things in the bedroom are not going the way they want them to go. For me it is very frustrating."

"I know you can't tell me everything, and even if you could, I don't think I could help you very much. Did the word divorce come up in the conversation?

"Yes."

"Oh my, things must be serious between them. Tony, I believe like so many things, that God will work things out for Bob and Ruth, and will tell you what you need to do. It has always worked that way and I have complete faith that the Holy Spirit will guide you in this matter. Tony, just put it in God's hand and ask him for wisdom. Wisdom will come."

"Thank you sweetheart, you seem to always know what I need."

18

1968

Tony was watching the six o'clock news on KING TV while Betsy was busy in the kitchen preparing dinner. The lead story was the war in Viet Nam and the horrible body counts. It seemed to Tony that every day the body count got bigger and the killing expanded to unbelievable proportions. These were the stories of men at war. They were stories about the horrors of fighting in the jungle not knowing where or when the enemy would open fire. They were stories of soldiers who did not know in the morning if they would live to see the sunset. Not knowing who the enemy is or what they looked like: The enemy could be the next child approaching you on the street; it could be the next young woman you meet, it could be anyone. You didn't need to confront a soldier to die. Anyone you meet could do the job.

Tony found it difficult to watch the reports and listen to the stories, but he felt compelled to listen. His heart went out to the young men who were drafted and sent to fight a war they didn't understand. They were pulled from the farms and homes of America and sent to a place most of them couldn't find on a map. For what? To kill someone. To kill the so-called enemy. To kill another human being. To kill. That's why there was a daily body count proudly announced on the evening news. We were told the more we could kill the sooner the war would be over. During World War II, General LeMay said, "If you kill more of the enemy than they can kill of you, you will win." Apparently, some folks still believed that garbage.

Gary, a young member of the church, was drafted right after finishing high school. He was only nineteen when he completed basic training and sent to Viet Nam. He was only there for three months when he was killed. He had been leading his squad on a search and destroy mission, in the point position. The point person was usually the first to die when they encountered the Viet Cong. The point was similar to the canary in the mine. When it died, the miners knew the air was bad and something was wrong. His letters home were filled with fear and homesickness. He longed for home, a place where he would be safe. This ghastly place was filled with death.

His first duty upon arrival was to work in the morgue. The dead were brought in from the field in body bags. Some of the bags contained entire bodies, badly disfigured by the fatal wounds, but many contained only pieces. Bags full of parts of human being who had given their lives for nothing. They had died because the other person killed them before they could do the killing.

It ate at Gary's soul. It went against every teaching he had received at home and in church. He went to work in the morning and sorted body parts. A head, a couple of arms, two legs and maybe some other parts were thrown into a casket and shipped home, under the name of a fallen soldier. Every day he was sick, couldn't eat, and vomited frequently. One of the men told him to get drunk for breakfast and if he could stay drunk all day, the work wasn't half so bad. He couldn't get drunk because that also went against his life's training and religious teaching. After two weeks, he was relieved of his duty in the morgue and sent to his regular outfit. It was now time for him to do the killing.

The new comers were scared and looked to the old-timers for help and direction. If you had been out in the field and lived, you were an old-timer. No one wanted to talk about the war they were fighting and their doubts and fears were kept bottled up inside, ready to explode at the least provocation. Alcohol and drugs of every kind were readily available. All you needed was the money and you could buy anything you wanted. Gary didn't use alcohol or drugs, but he prayed a lot. Guys laughed at him but he didn't care. He knew that only God, not booze and drugs, could get him through the year ahead. He laid out his feelings in his letters home.

The parents could hardly believe the letters they received. They took them to the local congressional representative but to no avail. The answer was always, "There's nothing we can do. The local commanders have to deal with the problems." But few ever did. When the burden became too heavy to endure, they brought the letters to Tony and Betsy. There was little they could do but to pray with the parents, and listen to their anguish.

When notice arrived of their son's death, it was almost more than they could bear. They both sat with Tony and Betsy and grieved. Both were unable to cry, unable to understand anything, especially how God could have allowed this to happen. Their son was a model young man, and his life had been taken by a war that was not understood by either of them, perpetuated by a government they could not persuade to stop. How could a God fearing nation of Christians allow such a war to continue and even expand? Where was their God? What was He thinking? Why was He not intervening and bringing this senseless war to an end? But above all, why had their God taken their son? Tony and Betsy tried their best to help them, but they both knew there were no answers.

*****

There was news of soldiers being spit upon and insulted when they returned home. Most of them didn't volunteer to serve; they had been drafted by their government and told to go. Now the people, who were able to avoid the draft, hated them and called them baby killers and murders. Everywhere you looked, things were upside down. The country seemed to be losing its mind. Veterans were homeless, unable to find a job, unable to find the help they needed to rid them of their anguish and demons from all of the death and killings they had endured. Many of them brought drug addictions home with them and alcoholism was rampant. These soldiers needed help, but the government that had sent them into this war had abandoned them. At least that's how it appeared to them.

Tony and Betsy were distressed by the news and prayed for God's guidance. Was there anything they could do? God answered in the form of a letter from the US Army's head chaplain, explaining the shortage of chaplains in the Army. If Tony was interested in becoming a chaplain in the US Army, he should call the number listed in the letter. They both knew immediately that this letter was an answer to their prayers, and that it was what God was calling them to do. They had to answer the call.

Tony contacted the church's District Superintendent and told him of his desire to become an Army chaplain. The district office was pleased with his decision and said that he would receive their support. They also asked Tony to delay his move until they could find a replacement pastor for the church in Burlington. Tony agreed, but then came the problem of explaining to his church why they wanted to leave. It would not be an easy task.

Tony called the number in the letter and made a commitment to join the Army as soon as a replacement pastor could be found. It would be a few weeks before they could leave their church and make the move. The Major who spoke to Tony knew all about that, because it had only been a couple of years since he himself had to leave his flock and make the transition to chaplain.

"We do this in almost every case so don't worry. We will stay in touch until you have a firm date and then we will make a plan. In the mean time, would you be willing to report to the induction station in Seattle and take a physical? If you can't pass the physical you won't have the problem of finding a replacement pastor," the major explained.

Tony immediately agreed and was given a date to report to Seattle. Betsy drove him to Seattle on that day, and he was given a complete and thorough examination. He passed with flying colors. There would be no medical problem standing in his way. Tony was sure this was God's will because of the ease with which things were moving. Now he had to tell the folks in the church.

* * * * *

The first person he called was Sister Judith Yardley, chairperson of the committee that served as the liaison between the pastor and the congregation. At first, she was shocked and then she cried, but soon agreed that God worked in His way and sometimes it was not how we expected or desired.

"Why?" Was her first question.

"That's easy to answer. Just watch the evening news. Those young men are being put into terrible circumstances, and they need the Lord more than ever. I feel strongly that God is calling me to bring them some comfort in their time of need."

Judith could only agree. "I'll notify the committee members, and I am sure they will want to talk to you about this."

The committee met with Tony and Betsy at the church, and of course, the first question was "Why?" Tony gave them the same answer he had given Judith, but got a different response from some of the members.

"Those men are killing women and children. They are burning villages and killing innocent people. How can you possibly want to go over there and provide them comfort?"

"They are not killers!" Tony replied, a little more forcefully than he intended. "They were drafted into the Army and sent over there to do what the officers and leaders tell them to do. They do not have a choice in what they are doing. I know, deep in my heart, that they don't like what they are told to do any more than you do."

"Maybe so, but I'm not convinced," was the reply. "Aren't you happy here in Burlington? Is there something we have done that makes you want to leave us? We just don't understand."

"Oh my dear brothers and sisters, there is nothing you have done to make us want to leave. You are all so dear to us, you are like family. But we both feel God calling us to do this. We feel it in the very fiber of our souls. We cannot say no to the call. Please understand that we love you, but we love God more and it is His call that we must honor."

The session was ended with that, and Tony and Betsy left. The committee members stayed for a while longer to pray and to talk about getting another pastor. They were all convinced that they would never find another pastor like Tony, but they had no choice but to try.

* * * * *

It took a few weeks but a new pastor was found and they could make arrangements to leave. On the appointed day, both Tony and Betsy went to Seattle where Tony was sworn into the US Army. They would spend the next twelve weeks in training. Both of them knew nothing about the army and nothing about being "an officer and gentleman." They also had no idea what it meant to be a chaplain and how it would be different from serving a civilian population.

During this time, Tony was on duty twenty-four hours a day. Betsy was called in periodically to attend training sessions on how to be a chaplain's wife, but mostly she stayed in their quarters and took care of the twins. There was much they both had to learn but after a few weeks, they were starting to get the feel of things. At the end of twelve weeks, Tony was given his chaplain badge and was pinned as a Captain in the U.S. Army. Tony's time as a pastor was taken into consideration and prorated to determine his rank. Because of this, he was given the rank of Captain. Even though he was told that he would not have to be directly involved in the fighting, he was given small arms training. He was required to qualify with a carbine and a hand held weapon. He hoped that he would never be required to use either of them.

Their first assignment was Fort Lewis, Washington. What an eye opener it was.

Lyle E. Herbaugh

* * * * *

Men were returning from the war. The wounded were sent to Madigan General Hospital for treatment. Madigan Hospital was well equipped and staffed for the treatment of this type of patient. It was the largest Army medical center on the west coast, and was assigned some of the best surgeons and medical personnel the Army had to offer. Madigan hospital was able to provide excellent care for the physical injuries of returning soldiers, but they were poorly equipped to deal with the "walking wounded" who returned with the condition commonly called "Shell Shocked." This condition was first recognized during the First World War, but was not well understood. Some called it Battle Fatigue. It was not widely treated as an illness, but more like a physical condition which would improve once the stress of the war had been removed. In most cases, it did not get better, and now it was affecting veterans all across the nation. The person most commonly involved in the treatment of this condition was the chaplain.

Tony talked with soldier after soldier, and heard the same story from each. The constant fear that was associated with combat wore them down until they became automatons, and ceased to feel. Upon returning home, they found it difficult to adjust to family life. Their wives couldn't understand what had happened to the men they loved. The children didn't recognize the men they called daddy. These men poured out their hearts to Tony. He listened, but he did not understand. He had never experienced the stress of combat. He could intellectually understand, but he could not relate to their problems and he could not feel their pain. He was at a loss as how he could best help them, so he did what he could.

He prayed with them. He quoted scripture and explained God's love for them. He tried to make them understand that God did not hold them accountable for fighting a war, and for killing a fellow human being. What they were feeling was not God's way of punishing them. This was not their fault!

Every day Tony made a trip to Madigan Hospital and visited the wounded. Over and over, he heard their stories of the horrors of war, and of things he could not even imagine. He tried to comfort the distraught and help the wounded feel comfortable. He assured them that they had not abandoned their comrades by getting wounded. None of their pain and suffering was their fault. He became more frustrated with every visit.

* * * * *

Tony brought his problems home with him and expressed his frustration to Betsy. They prayed together. They prayed for wisdom. They prayed for healing of the wounded. Nothing changed.

One evening, he and Betsy had just finished dinner and were washing the dishes. Tony often helped, because it gave them a break from the children, and for a few minutes, they could talk. This evening Tony had just finished expressing his frustration when Betsy said, "Maybe you should volunteer for duty in Viet Nam."

Tony was speechless.

Betsy continued. "You say you can't understand the men you are trying to serve because you can't visualize the conditions they are describing. You can't imagine the stress of knowing that when you get up and see the sunrise in the morning you might not see the sunset that evening. If you go and see firsthand what is happening, you will know and you will understand."

"I can't leave you and the family for a year. That is out of the question." Tony immediately responded.

"Think about it, Tony. God called you to help these men and women. He didn't put a restriction on his call, and tell you that you should only serve in Fort Lewis. He will protect you and keep you safe."

"Betsy, I can't do that."

"Yes you can, Tony. Don't make up your mind right now. Pray about it. Talk to the head chaplain about the duty, and find out what an assignment there would entail. Once you have done all this, you will know if it is God's will or not. I hate the idea of you being gone for a year, but this is eating at your very soul and it will not go away. You feel that you are failing these men, and the feeling of guilt is getting worse. I see you every day and I can see the changes in you. I have prayed about it for weeks now, and I don't see any other way."

A week later, Tony went to the personnel office and volunteered for service in Viet Nam.

It took only two months for Tony to receive his assignment orders to Viet Nam. He immediately called his father and his sister Jean and told them where he was headed. They were concerned for his safety, but promised they would write often and to pray for him daily.

It was a tearful goodbye at the airport with Betsy and the children. Their hearts were heavy and filled with fear that they had made a mistake in volunteering. It was too late to turn back now, so they prayed together for one last time and then Tony boarded the plane.

19

1969–1970

Somewhere in Viet Nam.

Dear Betsy,

I arrived safely. It was a long flight because we needed to stop, refuel, and change flight crews several times. Since we crossed the International Date Line, I am not sure what date we have or what time it is. All I know is that local time does not match my internal clock. Talk about time lag, believe me it is real.

Overall, the flight was ok. As you know, I had never flown before so everything was new and interesting; at least for the first few hours, then it became very boring. The noise from the four engines was so loud that conversation was difficult. The vibrations of the plane made it difficult for me to read, so I passed the many hours away by thinking about what we have done and about whether or not I am doing the right thing. When we signed up for service in the Army, I was convinced we had done the right thing, but now doubts are creeping into my thoughts.

When I arrived in Tan Son Niuht Air Base, the heat, humidity, and the noise and confusion, was almost overwhelming. Planes were landing and taking off, helicopters were circling over the base and in the distance, I could hear an occasional explosion. I have no idea what the explosions were, but they did not give me a warm fuzzy feeling. The guys who have been here for a while don't seem to notice them, so I assume, I hope rightfully so, that they do not pose a danger to us here on the base.

I am being called to attend an orientation, so I will stop for today. I will try and write something every day, even if it is just a few lines. God will take care of me, so don't worry about me. I will be fine.

I love you more than anything on earth. Kiss the kids for me.

Love, Tony.

* * * * *

Dear Betsy,

I learned today that I will not be staying here at TSN but will be moving to a forward base a few miles north of here. It is a rather large facility so I will be working with three other chaplains. A Catholic Priest, a Jewish Rabbi, and an Air Force captain who is a Protestant like me. Each of us will have a chaplains' assistant, who is an enlisted person. They will be assigned to each of us, and will travel with us at all times. I don't know what we will be doing and how services will be conducted, but I know we will soon find out.

The food here is plentiful, but not very tasty. We have reconstituted eggs for breakfast, and plenty of powdered milk to drink. There is constantly coffee available. If you think I made strong coffee at home, you have never drunk army coffee. I have to add plenty of milk and sugar to make it drinkable.

I have to go now. Until tomorrow.

I love you and miss you more than you can imagine. Write when you can. Somehow, we will get through this. Kiss the kids for me, and hold them tight for me. Tell them how much I miss them and how much I love them.

Love Tony.

* * * * *

Dear Betsy,

I settled into a temporary office today. It's not much to brag about, but it will do for now. I met my assistant. He is a young sergeant who truly loves the Lord. He was or, I should say, is against war and killing, but he felt the call of God to serve the men who must fight. He was drafted right after graduating from school and is only nineteen. Oh yes, his name is Ron James. I have to get used to him having two first names, but it shouldn't be too difficult. We immediately liked each other and I am confident we will be able to work well together.

Lyle E. Herbaugh

I held my first service today. We don't pay any attention to what day it is or what time it is. We are available to meet the needs of the troops. Not all of the chaplain staff sees it that way but most of us do. It was about two p.m. when some of the men from a forward base arrived. They are outward bound, going on ten days of rest and relaxation or R&R. Several of them wanted a chance to worship and relieve some of the tension they felt from combat. It wasn't a service like any you have ever seen me conduct. We sang a song that one of them suggested. I read some scripture, and I listened to them talk and then we prayed together. Most of them seemed relieved, and smiled when they shook my hand as they departed. I told them to have a wonderful time on R&R and hoped that I would see them again.

People come and go through here so often and so fast that I doubt that I will ever see any of them again, at least not here. It is possible, I suppose, that when I get to my duty station some of us could meet again. I have already been told not to make any serious friends or close relationships, because it only makes the loss more intense when they are killed or wounded. It just seems so unnatural to reject a friendship out of fear, but that is what most of the soldiers do. I feel I have a lot to learn.

I love you very much, and miss you and the kids. Give them all my love and kiss them for me.

Love Tony

DOUBT AND REDEMPTION

* * * * *

Dear Betsy,

We moved up to our new home today. We traveled as part of a convoy delivering supplies. Everyone was armed, we were led by an armored vehicle, and another one followed closely behind. We never stopped for anything, because no one knows when or where an attack will originate. The Viet Cong also plant land mines in the road, so every time you venture outside of a base or compound you are in danger. Today, we made it without incident. The Lord had his hand on us and protected us. I believe that He will continue to do so.

During the orientation briefing, we were told never to write a letter telling where we are located or what organizations are assigned to that location. This type of information can be of benefit to the enemy, so I'll just have to keep you in the dark as to my whereabouts. I would love to tell you every detail, but I can't. It would endanger everyone on the station, and I am here to comfort, not endanger folks.

Most of the enlisted men live in tents in groups of six or eight men per tent. The name they lovingly call them is hooch. I don't know the origin of the word, or even what it means, but it's their home for now. I think it is a slang word for a cheap hotel, but I'm not sure. They eat in a dining tent, and shower in a makeshift facility where they can get clean but not relax. The hot water is never available but a cold shower is welcome in the heat and humidity.

Right now, it's the rainy season and there is mud everywhere. The trucks and other vehicles keep everything muddy. I hear that it rains for nine months and then is hot and humid for the other three. The Lord told us that He would never put us in a position in which we could not endure, and I put my trust in Him.

Keep all of us in your prayers. I love you more each day. Do not worry about me. I will be safe. Hug and kiss the children for me, and tell them how much I love them.

Love, Tony

* * * * *

Dear Betsy,

Ron James and I moved into our permanent office today. I use the word permanent very loosely, because the building is a temporary building. It was hastily put together to provide a place to hold meetings. Then another one was built and this one was converted into offices to house all the chaplains and their assistants. It is dry, and comfortable. Being a captain gives me officer privileges, so we don't have to sleep in a hooch, but have actual buildings to live in. I don't feel very comfortable about that because I would like to live like the men I am here to serve, but for now, I am going to enjoy the luxury of having a real roof over my head.

I conducted a service for the men, but not too many attended. They don't like to be in large groups, because that presents too much of an inviting target for the Viet Cong. They prefer to talk to me one-on-one. Even here on the base, you never know who the enemy is. There is a constant flow of indigenous personnel on the base doing all sorts of jobs. There are housekeepers for the men in the hoochs, picking up and delivering laundry, and numerous other tasks. There have been incidences of a trusted houseboy sneaking a bomb on to the base and blowing it up in a hooch while the men were asleep.

If you listen to the names they call us Americans, and the crude and vulgar terms they use to describe us, I must wonder why we are here. The local population obviously doesn't want us here. Signs of "GI Go Home" are everywhere off base. I am told do not trust anyone, but I can't live that way. I trust the Lord to take care of me, and I cannot change that attitude.

I love you. Take care, and keep telling the children how much they are loved.

Love Tony

* * * * *

Lyle E. Herbaugh

Weeks pass.

Dear Betsy,

It is difficult for me to describe the conditions here. It's still raining. The mortar attacks are a regular nightly event. You can see the bright flash in the jungle outside the camp, and a few seconds later an explosion somewhere. Within minutes, the artillery opens fire pounding the jungle where the flashes were seen. That usually ends the incoming, which are not very accurate, but they make it difficult for the men to get any rest. When the shots are fired and the lookouts shout "Incoming" the men roll out of their beds and run to their assigned bunkers for protection. The attacks are usually only a few rounds, and most of the men don't even bother to get out of bed anymore. For the newcomers it is frightening and most of my business is made up of newcomers. They are scared and not yet jaded by the life they will endure for the next year, and that year seems like an eternity. They can only think that they will never survive that long. It takes a few weeks and sometimes months until they can bury the thoughts so deeply in their minds that they forget. They become robots, doing what they were trained to do. I fear the emotions they are burying will have long lasting effects on their young lives. I fear for their futures. Pray for them.

They come to me with stories of their fears, and their problems adjusting. They tell me about how their families are reacting to the war, and how bad it is at home. Some have brothers and sisters who have turned against them, and call them baby killers and other vile names. Betsy, you see what is happening on the nightly news, but I hear it up close and personal. This war is destroying our country, and there is nothing either of us can do about it but pray.

More to follow. I usually receive your letters in bunches, and it is so wonderful to read your words and see the pictures of you and the children. Every day that happens, it is a good day. Thank you. I love you so much.

Oh yes, my sister Jean and my father have been very faithful in writing and keeping me posted on their lives and activities. My other sister and my brother have also written several times. I must admit I sometimes find it difficult to write to all of them because I don't want them to worry about me, and the stories the men tell me are too horrible to repeat. I sit there with pen in hand and can't think of anything to write, so I tell them not to worry about me. I also tell them how much I love them. For now, that is the best I can do.

Kiss the children for me and tell them how much I miss them and how much I love them. I love you so much, and long to see your face again.

Love Tony.

* * * * *

Lyle E. Herbaugh

Dear Betsy,

Today I faced death for the first time. I won't give you too many details, but we were in route to a forward operating base when we came under fire. Even if it is only Ron and I who are traveling outside of the base, we are escorted by an armed vehicle. Usually it is a weapons carrier with twin 50 caliber machine guns mounted on the back. Today we were part of a convoy and making good time in spite of the poor condition of the road. We rounded a bend in the road when something near the front truck exploded stopping the truck and blocking the road. Small arms fire came from the woods near the road. The men jumped out of their trucks and returned fire. The twin 50s opened up with some withering fire at the place where the small arms fire had originated. Everything went silent. The damaged truck was pushed aside and we moved out quickly. Nothing happened until we arrived at the outpost.

We came to a stop and a young soldier ran up to our truck looking for the chaplain. He said that a couple of men had been seriously wounded in the incident, and were asking for a pastor. We ran to where the wounded men were and I saw that things were bad. A medical corpsman was working on one. The other just lie there with a look of panic in his eyes. I knelt beside him and took his hand in mine. I asked him if he believed in Jesus. He had difficulty speaking, but in his whispering voice, said that he had never been a religious person, but now that he was facing his creator, he had doubts. He didn't know if God would smile or frown when he arrived. He held my hand as we prayed together, me out loud, him silently. While I was praying, he died. I held his hand and cried like a baby. I had never seen death before, and this was not the way it should be. A young life gone without ever experiencing the peace that comes from knowing his Lord and Savior. Here was a young man, facing death, not knowing if he would be accepted into heaven or sent to the horrors of Hell.

At that moment, the memory of that sermon on Hell and eternal punishment, the one I had heard so many years ago, came crashing into my mind, and I rebelled against the thought. I could not believe any longer that our loving God would punish this young man who had just given his life in the service of his country by sending him to Hell. The whole idea of Hell and eternal punishment repulsed me. I suddenly no longer knew what I believed or what I should feel. I felt lost.

Pray for us all. I love you. Kiss the children for me. I miss you so much. It is times like this when I need to hold you in my arms and share everything with you. It is so difficult dealing with these things without your comfort which you provide so well. You are so precious and I love you more than life itself.

Love Tony

* * * * *

Months pass.

Dear Betsy,

Just two more months and I will be coming home. My time here has not been wasted. When I look back at the months and the hundreds of soldiers I have talked with, the places where I have conducted a worship service, the testimonies I have heard, where merely my presence made the men feel safer, I feel blessed to have been here with them. Maybe they were safer. God works in his ways and not human ways, so if I made them feel safer, I am thrilled.

We have held service in the field, setting up in the back of a truck. Wherever a small group of men could take the time, we would gather them together and worship. I had a dying soldier tell me that something I said and the reading of the 23rd Psalm, gave him comfort. The part where it is written *"I will walk through the valley and the shadow of death; I will fear no evil, for you are with me."* Gave him the courage he needed to hold on and continue to fight. It had given him comfort to know that God was there by his side.

The most common conversation I have is about the futility of this war. The news from home makes them think that everything they are doing is mindless and useless, that their brothers in arms are dying for no reason, and that nothing will come from their deaths. They admit that they don't want to be here but they are here. Their brother next to them doesn't want to be here either, but they are here and they fight to stay alive and to help their brothers stay alive. It tears my heart out to listen to them speak of their fears and their despair.

Some of the hardest things I must do are to officiate at memorial services. These men are bonded together through war and facing death every moment of every day, in a way that no one can possibly understand unless they have lived it. No civilian at home will ever understand. They can give it lip service but they cannot understand. When you are fighting side by side with a brother, and he is killed, a little bit of you dies with him. That piece of you that dies will never be resurrected. The scars will be there for the rest of your life, no matter how many times you pray to God and beg for His help, that piece of you is dead and it will stay dead.

These wonderful fellow human beings we are sacrificing on the altar of war will need help in the days and years to come. I fear that our government is not prepared to deal with the mental anguish with which these men will return home. They will need our help. The civilian population has so vilified these men that their lives will continue to be hell for years to come. Hatred and blame are vicious things that hurt so many people in so many ways. Our nation will have to change. We must return to our Christian roots of love and compassion. We must find it in our hearts to forgive and forget, before we can be healed. We must pray for our country and especially for the men and women who have served her so generously.

I love you, and I long for the day when I return to you and the children.

Love Tony

* * * * *

Dear Betsy,

I am back at Tan Son Nhut where I await my flight home. Part of the out-processing was a warning that we should wear civilian clothes when we arrive in the states, to avoid the ridicule that is heaped on the military. It is such a shame the way the military is being treated by those who are rich enough to avoid the draft. We have just fought a war with only the young and poor members of our society. I am ashamed.

I said good-bye to Ron James today. He left on a flight this morning. It has been a wonderful year serving with Ron. I told him how much I will miss him.

I will be returning to Fort Lewis, but I don't know how long I will be there. If possible, I will ask for Ron to be assigned to Lewis also. I still don't know fully how the Army functions. I suppose I never will.

I am mailing this letter, even though I hope to arrive before it does. I can't wait to hold you in my arms again. I love you, I love you, I love you.

Love, Tony

Lyle E. Herbaugh

20

1969–1970

Dear Tony,

You missed the big event, the twin's 5th birthday party. Several of the women of the chapel helped with the party, calling the other mothers and organizing the details of the day. We missed you. Martin cried when he learned that you would not be coming home for his birthday. He soon got over it when the other kids arrived with gifts for him. Carol Ann asked if you were coming, but when I told her that you were working, she accepted my answer and spent the rest of the party fully occupied with gifts, friends, cake, and fun. I missed you so terribly. When you are gone, it seems as if my very soul is missing.

We have established a routine in our lives geared to keep you fresh in everyone's memory. I keep an 8 by 10 photo of you wherever we are. It is on the table when we eat and every night when I tuck the children into bed, they hug your picture and say good night daddy. Then I go into the bedroom and cry for a little while. I cannot describe how deeply I miss you and how much I love you. If I doubted it was God's will, I couldn't stand it, but I know you are where God needs you to be, doing what He needs you to do, and I am content with that knowledge.

Be safe and come home to us soon. Write whenever you can find the time.

I love you.

Betsy, Carol Ann, and Martin

* * * * *

Dear Tony,

Last week I took the children to their first day of kindergarten. You remember where the school is situated and how we discussed this day. I wish you could have been here to share it. The school is only a few blocks from the house, and I am able to walk there in just a few minutes. School only lasts for half a day, so I pick them up at noon and we spend the rest of the day together. Being a mother is so wonderful, and since they started school, it is even better. Every morning when they are gone, I am able to do all of the little things that go into preparing a meal. I prepare everything so the actual time of making lunch and dinner is greatly reduced. I can also dust and vacuum the house, do the washing, and go shopping at the commissary, and not be slowed down by the two kids.

I always thought of kindergarten as a time for playing and socializing with the other kids, but it is much more than that. Yes, they do learn how to function with other children, which is much easier for Martin and Carol Ann because they have had to share everything since birth. Some of the others are an 'only child' and have never had to share or interact closely with anyone else. It is much harder for them, and I am sure, for their parents. The children actually learn things like their numbers and the alphabet. I think by the time they start first grade they will be able to read. Oh yes, they came home yesterday thrilled that the teacher sang a song that you always sang to them. It was the song about the itsy bitsy spider that went up the waterspout. They sang it all afternoon.

My time is taken up with all the little things that you used to do for me. By the time you get home, I might be an independent woman and you will have to fall in love with a new me. I pray every day that your experiences there don't change you in any negative way. I worry a little, because some of the wives of men who have recently returned complain that their husbands are different people. In some cases, it is tearing their marriages apart. I love the way you were, but if something changes, I will love you even more. Take care, be safe, and come home to us soon and whole.

I love you.

Betsy, Carol Ann, and Martin

* * * * *

Lyle E. Herbaugh

Dear Tony

That new washing machine we bought is a godsend. It is a big improvement over the old one and it washes cleaner, so my whites are white, and my colors are bright. I sound like a Tide commercial, don't I? I should have listened to you when you wanted to buy the matching dryer, but I was being a wise wife and wanted to save money, so I said we didn't need it. I should have known better, because we have lived here in Washington long enough to know that the weather is not conducive to drying clothes on a line. The bathroom constantly has wash hanging on that little rack which I put in the tub. By the time the children take their bath, things are dry and I can put them away, but it is an extra step required to prepare their baths. It is an extra step that would not be required if I had listened to you. Maybe I'm not the organized manager I thought I was.

Please don't worry about us. You have enough on your mind taking care of the men and women you are there to serve. We will be fine, but the living without you is not fine. We miss you so very much and I cannot describe how much we all love you. Be safe.

Love

Betsy, Carol Ann, and Martin

* * * * *

Doubt and Redemption

Dear Tony,

Today was not a good day for us here at home. Nothing happened to the three of us, but Helen Packard lost her husband yesterday. He was killed in action while on a search and destroy mission. She is a regular member of the post chapel. You may remember her. She is the tall red haired girl, maybe 25 years old. She loved to attend your services and loved the way you preached. We have been seeing a lot of each other and have become very close since you both shipped out for Viet Nam. They have a little girl who will never know her father. That alone is enough to make me angry, but to have him dying in a war that is so unnecessary makes it almost unbearable. How can we stop this madness?

I pray almost constantly for God to intervene and end the killing, but He remains silent. I am beginning to doubt the concept of God having a divine plan because I don't see a lot of evidence to support it. Things happen, and for anyone who has a loved one in the war zone, the happenings seem incompatible with a loving God being in charge. As strong as my faith is, I find it difficult sometimes. How much worse must it be for someone who is not a believer? For someone who has no God to hang on to. I shall not lose my faith, but sometimes I have doubts.

I love you so much. Stay safe and come home soon.

Love

Betsy, Carol Ann, and Martin

* * * * *

Dear Tony,

Someone heard me singing in church the other Sunday and asked if I would like to try out for the church choir. I did and I was accepted. We have been practicing once a week and I am really starting to enjoy it. I take the children with me and the chapel provides a baby sitter for the evening. Several others have older children who help out by playing with the younger ones. It is quite nice for all three of us.

The children have been attending Sunday school each week and have saved their work for you. Here are a couple of the lessons they completed over the last few Sundays. Each one is coated with their kisses and filled with love for you. In this house, you are truly loved.

In the next letter, I will send some pictures of the kids. We took them at church and they turned out nicely. You will be amazed at how they are growing. It seems like there is something new or a change that occurs every day. I can hardly keep up with the changes, so for you it will be a shock. I will keep photos coming whenever we take some new ones.

We love you and continue to miss you. Take care and be safe.

With love,

Betsy, Carol Ann, and Martin

* * * * *

Dear Tony,

Yesterday was not a good day for me. I went to the Lakewood Shopping Center to pick up some items while the children were in school. When I came out to the car, it wouldn't start. In fact, when I tried to start it, nothing happened. I started to panic because I was supposed to pick up the kids at noon and I didn't have a lot of time to spare. Since I talked you out of joining AAA to save some money, I had no one to call. I got out of the car, raised the hood, and stood there completely clueless as to what I should do, so I prayed.

A young man saw me and asked if I needed help. I told him my problem, and his immediate response was "I can take care of that for you. I see a Fort Lewis sticker on your car, is your husband assigned there?"

"Yes," I told him. "He is the chaplain and is presently serving in Viet Nam."

He was concerned and repeated that he could take care of my problem.

"How will you do that?" I asked, fearing that his solution might be expensive.

"I work at Jake's Auto and Body shop here in Lakewood. It is only a few blocks from here. I can go over there, pick up a new battery, and then help you install it. Would that work for you?"

I was so relieved that I blurted out that it would be wonderful. He looked at my battery and then left. In about five minutes, he was back with a new one. In another ten minutes, the new battery was installed and the car started immediately. When I asked him how much it cost, he told me that Jake was a Christian who practiced his religion in real terms. The battery was a thank you gift for our willingness to help the troops and to serve the country.

I can't help thinking that God had something to do with sending me that young man. He does indeed answer prayers.

I miss you, the children miss you, and we love you very much.

I send my love,

Betsy, Carol Ann, and Martin

* * * * *

Dear Tony,

It was another bad day yesterday. I had picked up the children from school, and decided I would visit Helen Packard for a few minutes. I think I told you that she lives in Lakewood on Mount Tacoma Drive. If I tend to repeat myself, please forgive me.

Anyway, I was driving up Bridgeport Way, when the right rear tire went flat. There was a pop and then the typical plop plop plop sound of a flat tire. I pulled into a parking lot of the little strip mall and stopped. That's when the real problem started.

I knew how to set the jack and lift the car, so I did that. I found the lug wrench and tried to loosen the lug nuts, but I was not strong enough to break them loose. The children were frightened and started to cry, which made matters worse. Once again, I stood by the car and prayed. Once again, God answered my prayers, and sent me help in the form of a military police sergeant. He was off duty and happened to see me standing there on the verge of tears.

When he saw the Fort Lewis sticker on the car, he also asked about you. When I told him whom you were and where you were, he got excited.

"I know your husband. You must be Captain Peterson's wife Elizabeth. I attend service at the chapel every week and I have heard your husband preach many times. He is a wonderful pastor. Now, let's take care of that flat tire."

It only took him a few minutes to change the tire and I was ready to go. He suggested that I go to Jake's Auto and Body shop to have the tire repaired. He knew Jake personally and said that he was a Christian. I told him about the battery and for a moment, I thought he was going to hug me.

I thanked him again, and went on to Helen's place. She is doing quite well, under the circumstances. Her parents, who live back east somewhere, want her to move there so they can be closer to the grandkids. I will continue to pray for her. Pray that the Lord will give her strength and help her make the right decision.

I love you and miss you very much.

We send our love,

Betsy, Carol Ann, and Martin

* * * * *

Dear Tony,

According to my count, it is only two more months until you return to us. We can hardly wait. It seems like a lifetime ago that you left to go overseas, but I know it is only 10 months. When I put it that way it seems easy, but for the children that is one fifth of their lives. That is a long time for them. They ask every night when you will be home. Your picture is smeared with their kisses and I don't have the heart to clean it. That little gesture of kissing their daddy is so precious to me, that I want to save it and somehow share it with you.

Things have been rather routine since my car problems. The school had a nice little party to celebrate the end of the school year, and the children's graduation from kindergarten. Both of them cried a little bit when I told them that there was no way that you could be there. It is so sad that you missed their entire kindergarten experience.

I have tried my best to be both mother and father for the past ten months, and I feel that with God's help I have done it well. It will be wonderful to have you here to share the burden with me. I shouldn't use the word burden, because the children are never a burden. They give so much joy and pleasure every day. What I am trying to say is that life is so much better when you are here.

I look forward to holding you in my arms soon. I love you very much.

We send our love.

Betsy, Carol Ann, and Martin

Lyle E. Herbaugh

21

Tony was only home for a few weeks and was just getting settled into the routine of peacetime service, when the Army head chaplain called.

"Captain Peterson, welcome home from the war. I heard many wonderful things about your service to the men in Viet Nam. You were an inspiration to many of the young soldiers. Thank you."

"That's nice to hear," Tony responded.

"That's not the purpose of this call though. Tony, I need you in Ohio!"

"Ohio? What is going on there that is so critical?" Tony asked.

"Do you remember back on the 4th of May when the students were shot and killed at Kent State? That was a terrible moment in the United States history. The young soldiers who were instructed to open fire on unarmed civilians are having a rough time adjusting. They had never shot at a human being before, and then to kill someone who was not a war enemy has been devastating to many of them. They need to draw closer to God, and the local National Guard Chaplains are over worked. Worse yet, none of them have any experience dealing with aftermath of killing someone. You have."

Tony was silent for a moment. He knew he had to go.

"How long will I be gone?" he asked. "My family will not be happy about this, but I guess I don't have a choice do I?"

"Yes Tony, I could direct you to do this, but I won't. You have had a long separation from your family, and I know this is asking a lot. Pray over it, call me tomorrow, and let me know what you decide. Thanks again for all you did for the troops in Nam. I look forward to your answer." The line went dead as he hung up the phone.

Oh dear Lord, Tony thought, *how do I tell Betsy that the Army needs me to leave home again. That she will need to be strong and be a mother and a father for a little while longer. She will not be happy about it.*

He only had one more year, and then he could leave the Army and return to a small church somewhere in Washington. He hoped it would be a church where he could stay at home and be a full time Father to his children. Right now, he was looking forward to it.

Betsy did not like the news, but she understood why the Army thought Tony was the only person who could deal with the situation in Ohio. She could feel the pain these young men must be suffering, knowing that they had shot and killed unarmed young people, who were no older than they were. To make it even worse, some of the kids who were killed were women. There would be no way in their minds that they could justify killing a girl for standing up for what she believed. The student riots that swept the country justified the killings in some people's eyes, but these men were "weekend warriors" not full time soldiers. They were well trained, but the act of killing an unarmed student on a college campus was not something for which their training could prepare them.

Tony stayed in Ohio for three weeks and was able to meet with the men involved. Not everyone was bothered by their actions and some didn't see a reason to talk to a preacher.

Doubt and Redemption

Those who wanted to, met with Tony on a one-on-one basis and they talked and prayed, which seemed to help several of them. Only time would tell.

Tony returned home feeling he had done the best he knew how to do. Life settled in to a normal routine. He was home with the children every evening. He helped them with their homework, he played games with them, and every night when he tucked them into bed, he gave them a hug and lots of kisses. How wonderful it was to be able to hold his children in his arms and hear them tell him how much they loved him. Life was, once again, great.

* * * * *

Tony had been in the Army for almost three years and the time was fast approaching for him to decide whether to stay in the Army or separate and return to his civilian church. He contacted the denomination's district superintendent to see if there were any churches available for which he might qualify to be head pastor. There were none in Washington or in Oregon, but he could be considered for several on the east coast. Both he and Betsy wanted to return to Washington, if it was at all possible, but they would take any location if they felt the call of God. They continued to pray for guidance and for discernment.

The children were in bed and the house was very quiet for a change, when Betsy raised the subject of their future. She wanted to know exactly how Tony felt about things and if he had any desires. Betsy had a way of getting Tony to open his heart and tell her exactly what was on his mind.

"Betsy I have been thinking and praying about this issue for a long time now, and I'm not sure I know what I want but I know what I don't want. Here in the Army we have been, for the most part, free of denominational doctrines and policies, and have been able to focus on the welfare of the men and women we are here to serve. It has allowed me to act in the way I felt God leading me without giving much thought to whether it fits the denomination's policy and procedures. It is a freedom I have come to appreciate."

Tony paused for a moment, staring off in the distance with a faraway look in his eyes.

"Even more important has been the freedom from petty bickering and in-fighting about how the church should be run. There has been a freedom from dealing with personality clashes and disagreements between people who should love each other. I sometimes think that I cannot go back to that way of living and I know I don't ever want to listen to someone tell me about his sex life. I really and truly don't miss that."

"Sure, in a civilian church, you get to know the folks and draw closer to them, and I miss the intimacy of those relationships, but intimacy also has its down side. It forces you to deal with another person's very personal issues and they expect you to have the answers to their problems.

Another positive aspect of a civilian church is that the members are not constantly changing. People come and go, but here in the Army, there is constant change and I seldom feel that I really know the members."

Tony paused for a moment and then continued. "There is another aspect of how I feel about this decision. I absolutely love the young men and women of the military. The idea of leaving them behind gives me the feeling that I am abandoning someone who needs me, and relies on me for some to the most important things in their young lives. What I feel is something a civilian cannot understand. Unless you have spent time with them, it is impossible to understand the affection I feel for them. I also interpret this feeling to be the manifestation of God's call."

Tony paused again, looked at Betsy, and asked her, "Now it's your turn. Tell me what you think and feel. How is the Lord leading you?"

"I believe that if God intended us to leave the Army and return to the civilian ministry, he would have provided a church for us. He didn't do that except on the east coast, and I definitely did not feel His call to go east. Our time in the Army has been quite satisfying and rewarding, except for the year you were in Viet Nam. Whenever I ask God for His guidance, the first thing that pops into my mind is that we should stay and continue to serve the men and women of the military. I feel that it is His way of telling me what we should do."

"Thanks Betsy. I am glad you have those feelings, because the exact same thing happens to me. Whenever I pray, that is the answer that comes to mind. Since it is happening to both of us, we must consider it to be God telling us where He wants us to be. When I think of returning to a church and dealing with the petty issues I mentioned a moment ago, I feel a sense of panic. I have such strong negative feelings, that I don't think I can ever return to that life. Since we are both having the same feelings, I think I should start the actions to extend our time in the military. We may end up on a post somewhere we don't like, but that is also part of the military life. I will never be required to return to Viet Nam, and I don't think that will change.

"I don't think we need to mention the decision to the children, because they are too young to understand, and they have no memories of the church in Burlington." Betsy stated. Tony agreed.

The next day Tony went to personnel and signed an indefinite term of service agreement. He would be in the Army for whatever the future held, for better and for worse. Both Tony and Betsy felt a sense of relief and were at peace with their decision. The head chaplain was also very pleased, because keeping chaplains on active duty was becoming more difficult the longer the war lasted. The needs of the service would guide the Army in Tony's next assignments. Both Tony and Betsy knew that they would not be at Fort Lewis very long. The worldwide commitments of the US Army meant that frequent assignments were inevitable. This proved to be true for Tony. Three years after returning from Viet Nam, he was called by the head chaplain and asked if he would like to see Europe. There was a vacancy for his rank in Kaiserslautern, Germany. It would be a three-year tour of duty, and it was in a very desirable part of Germany. The answer was easy for them, and they were soon headed for Germany, and a whole world of new experiences.

The war in Viet Nam continued to rage. In 1972, the president ordered a massive bombing campaign against the North. At Christmas, that year Hanoi was almost destroyed by the constant carpet-bombing of the city. No one knew how many civilians were killed. Early the next year the military carpet-bombed Cambodia, only this time it was kept a secret from the American people. Again, the death toll of innocent civilians was unknown.

These events troubled Tony and Betsy and their desire to serve and help the returning men and women from the war zone intensified. They were acutely aware of the impact this was having on the ones ordered to participate in the attacks. Even in Germany, the war was evident. Soldiers returned from Viet Nam and within a few months were reassigned to Germany. Many of them had had no chance to heal from their tours of duty in Nam and needed help that only the Lord could provide.

Then in April 1975, just a few weeks after Tony's 39th birthday, the United States realized that it had lost the war and withdrew. The longest war in American History was over. There would be no more fighting, but the scars of the war were widespread. Not just the veterans of the war were affected, but the civilian population was also deeply scarred by the senselessness of that war, and by the fact that we were beaten by a tiny country hardly the size of one of our states.

When the war ended, Tony was transferred to the Pentagon where he spearheaded the efforts to meet the needs of the veteran population. Because of his experience as a battle-tested chaplain, with experience in the war zone, he was asked to work closely with the Veterans Administration. He was no longer preaching sermons to the troops or providing personal care. He was spreading the gospel by establishing ways to meet the needs of a suffering population. It was rewarding work, but both Tony and Betsy missed the closeness of being the pastor of a flock and longed for an assignment as post chaplain once again.

Lyle E. Herbaugh

22

"Dad!" Martin said, "You still don't get where I am or where I feel I must go. It isn't that hard to do, but you have to let go of some of your old ideas about God and how He works."

"It says in the Bible 'I am the way the truth and the life, no man comes to the father but through me'." Tony responded.

"That is true in your holy scripture, but what about the other writings in the world that are just as real and just as sacred to their believers? Their holy scriptures tell another story. How can you say that yours is true and theirs is not true? What proof is there of that?"

"There is no proof. I believe the Bible to be true, and I have faith that what it says applies to my life and me. It also applies to what happens to me after death. It is true because I have faith that it is so."

"So you admit that Christianity is not the only way to enter God's place? Call it heaven or nirvana; you can achieve it through believing, not necessarily in what scripture you believe?" Martin confirmed.

"No, I don't admit that. I only admit that I do not have proof to support what I believe to be true," Tony answered.

* * * * *

This was just one of many exchanges of ideas and beliefs that Martin and his father had. Martin had learned when he was very young that he could say anything to Tony as long as it was well thought out and was not one of the generalizations or stock answers so many people threw around. It was also mandatory for any intellectual conversation that emotion stayed under control. No attacking the other person's statement with comments like "Oh that's just stupid," or saying anything demeaning to the other. It was through this type of exchanges that both Martin and Carol Ann had learned to explore ideas and concepts that were outside of the narrow rigid church doctrines in which they were raised. In the past, there had been many such discussions.

* * * * *

The twins were born on November 19, 1964, and from the moment of their birth, they had been raised in the ways of the Lord. Tony and Betsy had prayed together every evening, and had included the children in this time of devotion. Each held one of the twins, with Tony usually holding Carol Ann and Betsy holding Martin. The evening devotionals were an integral part of the children's lives as they grew up. They continued well into high school. With other activities, sports and school events, it was not always possible for them all to get together. During these times, when the children were not there, both Betsy and Tony fervently prayed for the children and for their continued spiritual welfare. They were keenly aware that the world was changing in ways they could not understand and in ways, they did not like. They could only pray that the children knew enough and that their faith was strong enough to withstand the pressures and temptations that were now a part of life for the youth of the world, especially for American youth. Only time would tell.

Army brats, as the children of military families were commonly called, grew up with a move every few years. They spent three years in Kaiserslautern, Germany where they lived in Vogelweh housing and attended the Vogelweh Department of Defense School. Following this, when their father was transferred to the Pentagon in Washington D.C. they spent four years living in Virginia.

The needs of the service took Tony away from his family for weeks at a time. There were maneuvers, war games and many other requirements that took him away on temporary duty. Tony spent many hours studying for his Masters Degree. Even for a chaplain, education was important for promotion in the military. God had led Tony to this place and he felt it was his responsibility to do the very best he could and to accept whatever the Army needed him to do.

Betsy was always there to hold the family together and to ensure the children's needs were met physically, emotionally and spiritually. It was not always easy, but she believed as Tony did. That God had led them to the Army, that they must serve to the best of their ability and be content with whatever God gave them to do.

When the twins were 14 and ready to start high school, Tony was promoted again, and Lt. Colonel Peterson was once again transferred to Fort Lewis. They elected not to live on the post in Government housing, but instead, bought a house in the nearby town of Steilacoom. They were home again in Washington, back where it all began.

Western Washington was always a liberal part of the country. Early in its history there had been several communist communities settled there with the plan to socialize the entire state. It didn't happen and by 1915, most of these utopias had failed and died out. The liberal thinking remained and became a lasting element in the social and political structure of many of the communities.

The town of Steilacoom was settled sometime around 1854, and was one of the largest towns in early Washington. Tacoma and Olympia soon overtook it in size and importance, but Steilacoom remained a vibrant community. With the growth of Fort Lewis and McChord Air Force Base, during World War II and the Korean conflict, Steilacoom became a thriving bedroom community. In 1978, Steilacoom High School was ranked as one of the best schools in the country and was the school of choice for many of the military officers and their families. Martin and Carol Ann enrolled in the fall of that year.

*****

During their high school years, both Martin and Carol Ann were active in high school activities. Martin played football and basketball, making the varsity team as a starter. During his senior year, the Sentinels basketball team made it to the state tournament but did not win the title. The following year they became the state 1A champions. Carol Ann was not inclined to play sports because for girls, the choices were very limited. She did, however; enjoy acting and joined the drama team, playing lead roles in several school plays. Both of them were excellent students, making the honor roll all four years.

In their academic studies, they were exposed to unfamiliar ideas about how the world was created, based on the theories of evolution and science. From early childhood, they had been taught that the Bible is the word of God and that the answers to all of life's questions and problems could be found somewhere therein. They had accepted that the Bible was literally true and that it told the actual historical story of man and the universe. They had never stopped to think about the seven-day creation, or about how many years had elapsed from Adam to Jesus. They had accepted without question what they were taught in Sunday school. Now they were being told that the earth was several billion years old, that man was not created in the image of God, but that man had descended from apes. They began to question and doubt the things they had always thought to be true. They brought these questions home and discussed them with their parents.

"Dad," Martin began, "You never told us how long ago the world was created. You only said that God had created it along with everything else in the universe. Now science is showing us that it didn't happen the way Genesis tells us it did. How do you account for that? What am I supposed to believe?"

"I'm not real sure how to answer that question, Martin. Advances in science are making many of the old beliefs outdated, even some of the long held church teachings. I only know how I feel and what I believe to be true. You will have to decide for yourself, based on the facts and on the strength of your faith. I firmly believe that God did create man and everything in the universe. He set in motion all of the laws of physics and of nature that science is now unraveling and beginning to understand. How long ago He did this is not clear to me, but I firmly believe that God is responsible. Does that help a little?"

"Yeah, some. I also believe God is the creator, but the time span of creation may not be as I understood it to be when I was a child," Martin said questioningly.

"You may remember," Tony explained, "that in 2 Peter 3:8 it is written that *'to God, a day is a thousand years and a thousand years is a day'*. That puts a little different spin on things."

"Dad, it kind of bothers me that all this new stuff is being pushed my way and so much of it is in conflict with my early teachings. I am frequently at a loss for what to believe. My doubts about what I think I know and what I think I believe get stronger. Is it wrong for me to doubt? Is it wrong to question the validity of my prior beliefs?"

"No, I don't think it is wrong to doubt or to question certain truths. As you already know from science, every premise must be tested. You build a hypothesis and then test it to see if it stands. The same thing is true for most beliefs, even some religious beliefs, but you must be careful. You should never question if Jesus is our Lord and savior or that He died for our sins. Just about everything else is open for discussion. Always keep in mind that man cannot have two gods, and to many folks science has replaced God. You can use science to test and prove certain statements and philosophies. You can even test what certain scriptures say, but you can only believe in one God. When I say, believe I mean believe in your heart. To understand intellectually that something is so is not the same as believing it in your heart. You can say that you think it is true that Jesus died and rose again, but you must truly believe it deep in your being to be truly saved."

"Another thing that bothers me, Dad, is that my doubts will probably get worse the farther I go in my education. I plan to attend Stanford University and study math so I know I will be faced with many unanswered questions and unconfirmed theories. I don't quite know how I will handle that when I get there."

"Well Martin, you can always feel free to come to me. As you already know, I will not criticize you for not understanding or not knowing. I will always tell you what I believe to be true, but you must make your own decisions. That's one thing about your religious beliefs; no one can make the decisions for you. You must determine what you truly believe and then live with the decision. One other point: Upon close examination of the Bible, you will realize that there are very few things that we are told to do. First, love the lord with all your heart, and all your mind, and love your neighbor as yourself. On the negative side, there are only a few do not dos. Everything else is gray and open to interpretation."

"Thanks Dad. I know you have always been there for me when I needed advice or had questions, and I know that will not change just because I have grown up. You always know what I need. I really love you and thank the Lord often that He gave me you to be my father."

A similar discussion was going on between Betsy and Carol Ann. As the two children became adults, the intensity of the conversations increased, and the depth of the questions and answers increased as well. The one thing both parents understood was that they must be honest with the kids, and not try and force-feed them the religious dogma they had grown up with. The young people must determine what they find to be true and then make their own decisions. Both parents knew that there would be decisions and questions that would try their souls, but it was their responsibility to do what was right for the two children. They prayed for them every day of the year.

Lyle E. Herbaugh

23

In June 1982, the twins graduated from high school with honors. They were numbers one and two in the graduating class. Carol Ann was valedictorian and Martin was a very close second. Both of them spoke at the graduation ceremony. It was the first time twins had finished in the two top positions, and for both to speak at graduation. Tony and Betsy were very proud of the twins, and of their accomplishments.

Carol Ann was accepted at the University of California at Berkeley. She also received a sizeable scholarship. Her plans were to major in psychology with a minor in philosophy. She hoped one day to complete her Doctorate in Psychology and work in the mental health field. She was gentle and compassionate and had developed very good listening skills. Her high school counselors were very impressed and felt strongly that her choice was a good one.

Martin, on the other hand, wanted nothing to do with the humanities. He was totally into the fields of math and science. He received a four-year scholarship to Stanford University to major in math with a minor in mechanical engineering. It was time for the twins to leave the protection of home and for the first time, face life as adults.

* * * * *

In the fall, the twins left for college. Tony and Betsy drove them to their schools and helped them get moved into their dorms. After a long day of carrying boxes and suitcases up several flights of stairs, the day ended with dinner in a fast food restaurant, and then goodbyes.

For Betsy, it was the most difficult thing she had ever had to deal with. The year Tony was in Viet Nam was hard, but not having the children around her was almost more than she could bear. For the past 19 years, they had occupied much of her life. Every decision they had made as a family was based on the needs of the children. Of course, the call of God was number one in their lives, but what to do and how to implement that call always prioritized the needs of the twins over the needs of Mom. Given that Tony was required to meet the needs of the service, looking out for the welfare of the children often fell to Betsy. She had relished the task and accepted the responsibilities with a light and profoundly happy heart. She had examined the needs, prayed for wisdom, and made the decisions. Now the children were gone, out of her control, and she no longer needed to make decisions for them, or to tell them what to do or when to be home. She was lost. She felt much like a sailing vessel caught in the doldrums. The wind was gone. At times, she felt that her life was over because the focus of her life was gone, and she was adrift.

Tony also missed the twins a great deal, but his other duties kept him so busy that he had very little time to dwell on it. In the evenings, they talked about everything; including how Betsy felt about the "Empty Nest Syndrome" and its impact on their lives. It was soon clear to both that Betsy must find something to fill her life and give her a new focus. She had no desire to return to teaching so she looked elsewhere. Nothing seemed to fit. Finally, she doubled her volunteer time with the Ladies of the Chapel and kept as busy as she could. She didn't feel that she was depressed but the hole in her heart the twins had left was very real.

The twins came home for Christmas, and spring break, and then summer vacation. Every time they came home, they seemed different, a little more distant, and a little more independent. Both Betsy and Tony knew that it was supposed to be this way. The twins were no longer children, but adults, making their own decisions and choices. This was the time for the children to leave the nest and fly on their own, a time to untie the apron strings and to become adults. The knowledge that this was right for the twins did not lessen the emptiness Betsy felt.

A very difficult part of the process for Tony and Betsy was to watch the twins pull away from the Christian principles they had been so carefully taught. The principles Tony and Betsy had been given in their youth and had with a joyful heart, passed on to their children. Carol Ann was exposed to the writings of the great philosophers like Kant, Nietzsche, Carl Jung, Karl Marx, and Sigmund Freud., espousing different perspectives including, "God is dead." "There is a reason for everything, and it is not God." "Your dreams are your inner reality and they have nothing to do with God." She was also introduced to the teaching of The Buddha and was extremely impressed with the peace, love, and pacification of the Buddhist teaching. The reverence for all life forms moved her and fit well with her personality.

Tony had been exposed to these things when he was in school and it had provoked questions, but his faith was strong and he remained focused on God, and he had not lost his way. There had been very little outside peer pressure to draw him away. Carol Ann did not yet have that level of maturity and she was drawn away.

Martin found in science the answers he had searched for in the Bible. The answers were all there waiting to be deciphered and analyzed. The creation of the universe, the evolution of man, and the rest of nature were laid out for him. The principles of physics and the laws of nature he had believed were from God were not necessarily the way he had been taught. Science was slowly replacing God in his life and he experienced a feeling of relief. A relief from not knowing, a relief from doubting the validity of what he had been told. He found a peace he had never known before. His parents had insisted that their beliefs were right but Martin had always had doubts. He had accepted their teaching and those of the church but some doubt had always been present. Now he was sure he knew and understood and it gave him peace and satisfaction.

*****

When it was time for the twins to return to school for their sophomore year, Betsy was very surprised by her feelings. She was actually glad they were leaving and that she and Tony could return to the life they had learned to appreciate. As soon as Betsy had gotten over her feeling of loss, she and Tony found time to be with each other and to enjoy the quiet evenings with no thoughts or worries about where the kids were or when they would be home. Each time the twins came home from school, they were glad to see each other but after a few hours, both of them had friends to visit and things to take care of. The common goodbye was, "don't wait dinner for me; I don't know when I will be home."

When they were at home, talk often turned to their studies and the new idea or concept which had been revealed to them. Frequently the wonderful revelations were in direct conflict with their religious teaching and of course, the religious teaching fell by the wayside. Tony could deal with this logically and in a straightforward manner, Betsy, however; struggled with it. She couldn't help worrying about where she and Tony had gone wrong in their teaching of the children. They both drew comfort from the words of Proverbs 22:6 *"Train a child in the way he should go, and when he is old he will not turn from it."*

By the time she graduated, Carol Ann was a practicing Buddhist. She made time in her busy schedule to meditate. Meditation gave her peace of mind and calmed whatever it was in her life that was causing her stress. For her it was more of a health issue than a religious one. She was content with not having any religious dogma or Christian teachings to live by or to doubt. She found everything she needed in Buddhism.

Martin had become a very good scientist and in the transition found that science did not have all of the answers. In fact, science frequently raised more questions than it provided answers. Every once in a while he would return to the teaching of his youth and pray. The act of prayer actually gave him comfort. Sometimes, it was good for a man to give his problems to someone else to solve. He was not sure why that was, but whether he understood it or not, it seemed to work and he was not afraid to do it. He didn't, however; broadcast it to his colleagues, nor did he tell his parents.

Betsy and Tony continued to struggle with whom and what was to blame for the twins falling away from God. After years of blaming themselves, they finally decided that no one was at fault. There was nothing they should have done differently and there was nothing they could do now. It was totally in God's hands and they should give it up to Him and wait and see. Both of the children were of high moral character and lived their lives in accordance with the golden rule as stated in the bible. There was not one thing in their lives that could be criticized. In spite of this, or maybe because of it, both parents had doubts that either of the twins, as adults, had asked for forgiveness of their sins and accepted Jesus as their savior. The question they had asked so many times in their lives still haunted them. Was accepting Jesus as a child enough to guarantee salvation or could it be lost?

AFTERWORD

Tony retired from the Army with the rank of Colonel. He took a position of head pastor in a small church in the town of Concrete, Washington. The peace and quiet of the little mountain town was a welcome change from the hustle and bustle of Army life. Betsy remained the loyal wife and gladly served the congregation of Concrete.

After spending two years in India searching for the true path to salvation, Carol Ann returned to Berkeley and completed her Doctorate of Psychology. During her time in India, the filth and strange practices she encountered caused her to rethink her beliefs. Buddhism lost much of its luster and she returned to Christianity. She did not entirely abandon Buddhism; but combined the practice of meditation and Buddhism's respect for all life, with her Christian teachings and became a Buddhist/Christian. She is working in the mental health department of Swedish Hospital in Seattle. She is married to a fellow doctor and they have one daughter. She is very active in the community and is a member of a Universal Unitarian church.

Martin received his Ph.D. in Mathematics from Stanford. He is employed by the Jet Propulsion Laboratories in Pasadena, California where he is part of the team working on the Mars Rover project. They plan to have a remote controlled rover on the surface of Mars in the next ten years. Martin attends and is a member of a local Presbyterian church who regards church attendance as part of his community obligation. Many of his colleagues do the same. He is married to a fellow scientist and they have no children.

End

CPSIA information can be obtained
at www.ICGtesting.com
Printed in the USA
FSOW03n0830010515
6843FS